The Museum of Mysteries

Also from Steve Berry

Cotton Malone Novels
The Lost Order
The 14th Colony
The Patriot Threat
The Lincoln Myth
The King's Deception
The Jefferson Key
The Emperor's Tomb
The Paris Vendetta
The Charlemagne Pursuit
The Venetian Betrayal
The Alexandria Link
The Templar Legacy
The Bishop's Pawn
The Malta Exchange

Stand-alone Novels
The Columbus Affair
The Third Secret
The Romanov Prophecy
The Amber Room

Also from M.J. Rose

Tiffany Blues

The Library of Light and Shadow

The Secret Language of Stones

The Witch of Painted Sorrows

The Collector of Dying Breaths

The Seduction of Victor H.

The Book of Lost Fragrances

The Hypnotist

The Memoirist

The Reincarnationist

Lip Service

In Fidelity

Flesh Tones

Sheet Music

The Halo Effect

The Delilah Complex

The Venus Fix

Lying in Bed

The Museum of Mysteries

A Cassiopeia Vitt Adventure

By: Steve Berry and M.J. Rose

EVIL EYE
CONCEPTS

The Museum of Mysteries
A Cassiopeia Vitt Adventure
By Steve Berry and M.J. Rose

Copyright 2018 Steve Berry and M.J. Rose
ISBN: 978-1-948050-70-8

Published by Evil Eye Concepts, Incorporated

Dedicated to all of the talented writers of
1001 Dark Nights.
All are ladies extraordinaire
who, together, make magic happen.

Sign up for the 1001 Dark Nights Newsletter
and be entered to win a Tiffany Lock necklace.

There's a contest every quarter!

Go to www.1001DarkNights.com to subscribe.

As a bonus, all subscribers will receive a free copy of
Discovery Bundle Three
Featuring stories by
Sidney Bristol, Darcy Burke, T. Gephart
Stacey Kennedy, Adriana Locke
JB Salsbury, and Erika Wilde

"In this time of winter and destruction there were brave men among the Britons, striving with might and wisdom to preserve their country, to maintain an orderly and decent system of government, to preserve town, church, and villa, to rescue the beleaguered, and to bring peace to the land. Such a man was Arthur."

An anonymous ancient historian

Chapter 1

I RAN BAREFOOT AFTER THE THIEF.

But here's a life lesson.

Kitten heels and cobblestones don't go together.

Never have. Never will.

And since there was no way to avoid the treacherous ancient walkways, I just kicked off my shoes and kept going. Making matters worse, the narrow, wet street twisted upward in a brutal S curve, but I managed to keep the dark gray sweatshirt in sight as my quarry plunged through the few tourists who'd braved the nasty weather.

Eze was part town, part museum, part a-place-from-another-time. Its shops, galleries, hotels, and cafés attracted people by the busload from around the world. The oldest building dated to the early 1300s, the whole thing just a mere few acres and appearing like something created as an amusement park. The tourist office loved to boast that Walt Disney once spent a lot of time there. Why? Who knows. But I'd like to think it provided a bit of inspiration.

The tiered village nestled high in the clouds above the French Riviera, about halfway between Nice and Monaco, and carried a mystique that I'd always been drawn to. Writers likened it to an eagle's nest atop a rocky seaside peak. So many had tried to claim its valuable perch. First the Phoenicians, then Greeks, Romans, Italians, Turks, and Moors. By the 14th century the French had gained a firm hold and the House of Savoy fortified it into a stronghold.

From its 430-meter elevation above the sea, an enemy could be seen a day in advance of coming ashore. Its motto was particularly apropos. *In death I am reborn*. Its emblem was a phoenix perched on a bone. Not exactly Mickey Mouse, but the symbolism seemed to fit this charming piece of the past.

I kept running.

Thankfully, I stayed in shape. Not three miles every day, but at least every other. But that was usually on flat French terrain. This obstacle course was a different story. Still, I was gaining on the bastard.

And I'd get him.

The thief disappeared over a crest.

A black thunder cloud rolled across the sky. Rain continued to pour down in ever-increasing sheets, the water filling the drains at either side of the shiny cobblestones, rushing downward in two swift currents. A sharp flash overhead was followed by another thunder clap which rattled glass in the olden buildings. I came to the crest and started downhill, the winding twists working even harder against me.

News flash.

Bare feet and wet rocks don't mix either.

Gray Sweatshirt was wearing rubber-soled sneakers. New ones, I'd noticed earlier. Not a mark on them. Working like wings at the moment, providing sure footing. He was toting the knapsack he'd carried into the museum, which surely still held the wooden box. What a way to spend what was supposed to be a relaxing day with an old friend.

I wasn't sure of Nicodème's age. Maybe mid-eighties. I'd never asked, though he'd been around nearly my whole life. He was a gnarled, walking stick of a man with a face like the pummeled look of an unfinished sculpture topped by a mop of unkempt white hair. My father, doing what wealthy men did, had been a collector of rare coins, stamps, and books as well as ancient Egyptian and Roman glass and pottery. Nicodème had long been a dealer in all of those and visited us several times a year in Spain, always bringing curiosities for my father's perusal, staying with us a few days, telling stories of the world, then leaving with more money than when he'd arrived.

Knowing how much I loved perfume, he never failed to bring me a flacon of some kind. My favorite was still the tiny quartz bottle with a black jade stopper that hung from a silver chain, which I wore often. Opened, I could catch a whiff of the original formula it had once held. I'd never filled it with anything else for fear of losing that faint suggestion of that long lost scent. My curiosity about scents began as a child when my mother gave me my first bottle of cologne. A light floral lemon with a hint of orange blossom. *Expectations*. A curious name.

But one I never forgot.

A jolt of pain surged up my right leg.

Dammit.

Something had bruised the bottom of my foot. Aware of the fragility of ankles and the price of stumbling, I slowed and reached down, applying pressure which resulted in more pain.

No choice.

I kept going.

More of that self-discipline I'd taught myself through too many life lessons and bad decisions to count.

My target remained in my sights about thirty meters ahead. I stumbled on a cracked cobble and nearly lost my balance, but I wasn't going to stop. This thief had stolen something invaluable. How did I know that? Nicodème's instructions as I'd bolted from the shop.

Get it back. No matter what.

His air of urgency unmistakable.

Nicodème's shop sat at the end of one of Eze's oldest streets, against the outer wall, pressed to the mountain, where not all that many tourists ventured. The thief had knocked, entered, and examined what he'd come to see—a wooden box waiting for him on the counter. He was polite and asked intelligent questions. Which raised no alarm bells, as antique dealers were the shop's main customers.

He even provided a name.

Peter Hildick-Smith.

Nicodème never advertised and no signage identified the building or business other than a bronze number 16. The door stayed locked and all visits were by appointment only. Hildick-Smith had scheduled his last week, there to see some of the ancient glass, as he'd heard Nicodème stocked quite a bit.

Which was true.

The display cases were filled with rare antique bottles, glasses, bowls, jugs, and jars. Differing styles and craftsmanship from around the world. The shelves were stacked with catalogs and books about glass, pottery, and carved stone. A reference library any museum would be envious to own. Hildick-Smith, though, had come to see something in particular, something that he'd confirmed was there at the time of the appointment.

A wooden box.

Rectangular shaped, fashioned of shiny rosewood, the cover inlaid with cabochon stones—amethysts, moonstones, garnets, and sapphires.

From the back of the shop. In what Nicodème called the Museum of Mysteries.

Where access to the front was by invitation, only people who possessed treasures Nicodème was trying to acquire, or scholars who harbored information about treasures already ensconced, were invited into the museum itself. Few of the locals living in Eze knew the stone house and storefront, located at #16 on Rue de Barri, harbored a secret museum. Nor did they know that the elderly antique dealer, Nicodème L'Etoile, was also a mystic whose passion was collecting supposedly powerful and sometimes dangerous portents from the past.

I even knew of a few.

Things like a portrait, drawn by da Vinci in chalk created from mummies, which bestowed great physical power to anyone who gazed upon it. Greek fire, invented in the 7th century by the Byzantines, that produced a flame water was unable to quench. A collection of evil eye talismans that dated back to ancient times, said to have belonged to witches. And the Spear of Destiny that Charlemagne, Napoleon, and Hitler believed turned an ordinary man into a superhuman leader. When I'd pointed out that there was already such a spear on display at the Hofburg in Vienna, he'd merely smiled and said *beware of fakes*.

The L'Etoile family traced its roots back to the 13th century. The name carried a popular familiarity thanks to a branch of the family that came to fame in the early 18th century as perfumers to royalty. L'Etoile fragrances became known worldwide and their shop on the Left Bank in Paris remained one of the most famous perfume destinations in the world.

And one of my personal favorites.

Fifty years after the French Revolution one member of the family, Sebastian L'Etoile, settled in Eze, opening a shop to sell his brother's fragrances. Eventually, he branched out and founded the Museum of Mysteries, mainly as a place to store artifacts brought back from expeditions to Egypt. Sebastian rediscovered a tunnel that extended from the back of the shop into the mountain, closed off long ago by an avalanche, perfect as a repository. So an entrance was created from the shop. A door, with no knob, no knocker, no lock. Just oak panels bound by iron. Which only the curator could open through a complicated puzzle that predated Sebastian L'Etoile's rediscovery.

Curiosity had gotten the better of me, and so some research had revealed that, in the 5th century, some of the women of Eze, after being branded witches, had used the tunnel as an escape route down to the sea. Their stories were told through carvings in the walls, which Nicodème had allowed me to see. Goodbye messages. Parting advice. Recipes for spells and potions. Final messages to those they were leaving behind. Seeing them at once both moving and hopeful. Now the old tunnel contained over three hundred rare objects.

One of them apparently gone.

Being carted away, through a rainstorm, across the streets of Eze by a thief.

Hildick-Smith hung a left at a fork in the street, which gave me hope. I knew Eze, every warren of turns and alleyways, every dead end. Clearly my quarry wasn't as well versed since he'd just chosen one of the inescapable routes, this one ending at a viewing platform where tourists could gaze at the valley below, the towns in the distance, and the endless sea and sky.

I took the same left and saw Hildick-Smith ahead.

He stopped running, then casually joined a small group of visitors with umbrellas enjoying the scenic vista. I slowed, caught my breath, and approached. To gain control of the wooden box, Hildick-Smith had drawn a pistol in the shop and held both me and Nicodème at bay. If threatened, he might use his weapon. My instincts told me to shout for the people to clear out so I could deal with the problem. But approaching I suddenly realized something.

He was gone.

But how?

I reached the railing and looked down at the twisty footpath about three meters below. I knew that it led from Eze down to the sea, about a ninety-minute trek. The dubious Philosopher's Walk. Legend held that the famed German, William Nietzsche, would hike the zigzagging path among the trees every day in summer. The exercise and heat supposedly providing inspiration to organize his thoughts. Beyond its edge was a sheer drop down of several hundred meters. Today, the danger was amplified by steel-gray rain slanting down through the trees.

I saw Hildick-Smith, clutching the knapsack to his chest, navigating the stone-riddled path. Not running, but definitely hurrying in and out of the trees. I followed suit, doing what he'd obviously done, and hopped the railing, landing on more hard rock.

Which hurt my bare feet.

I headed after him, the shock of each stride sliding up through my bones, the pain tearing into my lungs, heart hammering, the sucking of each breath beginning to match the beat of my legs. I could only imagine the condition of the bottom of my soles.

Ahead, my target disappeared as the twisty path continued its descent. The storm seemed to have scared off all other hikers. At the next bend there was no sign of him. No movement anywhere. Just the hills, the trees, the sea beyond, and the rain overhead.

He has the elixirs.

That's what Nicodème had said as I left.

What elixirs?

I'd come to Eze simply to have lunch with an old friend. It was our special thing. About once a month, whenever I was home in France, not traveling. My passion was the rebuilding of a medieval castle using only 13th century materials and technology. I have degrees in medieval architecture, so the design was my own. Every meter of the thick walls and corner towers had been fashioned by hand from the nearby water, stone, earth, sand, and wood. I employed quarriers, blacksmiths, masons, stone hewers, potters, and carpenters who worked year round. The costs were enormous. Luckily my parents left me with more money than I could ever spend. So I'd decided to put some of it to historical use. And I was making progress. About thirty percent of the castle now stood, but it would take another twenty years to finish.

Which was fine.

It wasn't the destination, but the journey that interested me.

The drive from my home in Givors to Eze was several hours, but it was lovely through the Côte D'Azur region, the Alps rising on one side, the Mediterranean stretching out on the other. My visit today had a dual purpose since Nicodème had told me that he'd acquired some exquisite 15th century tiles that he thought might be perfect for one of the buildings. He'd helped me many times over the years with the castle. I appreciated his interest as his suggestions were always on target.

"What is this?" I had asked, pointing to the wooden box on the counter before Hildick-Smith arrived. *"It looks like something my father would have loved."*

"He would have. The box itself is medieval, probably 13th century. But what's inside dates back much further. It's filled with ancient potions used by healers."

"Witches," I'd whispered.

The *wise women* had always interested me—maligned by men who didn't understand their talents, sexuality, or intelligence. Not witches. Merely observant experts in the healing arts, which had far more to do with chemistry than magic. I'd borrowed a few books from Nicodème's shelves over the years about the dark arts and its various practitioners. What was the most common charge from the time? *As a ghost, they appeared and disappeared.*

Just like Hildick-Smith.

What was happening here? That wooden box? Elixirs?

"This could be a most important item," Nicodème had said to Hildick-Smith, touching the lid of the intriguing box.

"I heard you acquired it a few years ago. So I came to see if you would sell it to me."

"I'm afraid not."

"I'll double what you paid for it."

"It is not for sale."

A moment later Peter Hildick-Smith drew a gun, took the box, and fled the shop.

Now he was gone.

Chapter 2

I CREPT AHEAD.

Through the years I've honed a few instincts, the kind that come from chasing trouble. I've always liked trouble. Why? Hard to say. Maybe because it's so unpredictable. So spontaneous. The knowing, but not knowing. It's what lies ahead that makes life interesting.

I'm a glass-half-full kind of girl. Nothing to be gained by always looking at the sour side of things. It probably comes from a rich, affluent upbringing. I wanted for little. My parents were billionaires, but they were no coddlers. My father was tough, my mother tougher. They were also Mormon, converted in middle age, which instilled in them a deep sense of duty and responsibility. They were firm believers and, at the time, there weren't all that many Latter-Day Saints in northern Spain. Being different was an open invitation to trouble. But my father had never been afraid of trouble either. He actually seemed to thrive in its presence. So it's no surprise that I turned out the way I did. By the time he died, the local Mormon ward numbered in the thousands, all thanks to him.

Thoughts of him always kept me going when trouble arrived.

Like now.

I came to the next bend in the Philosopher's Walk, which inched ever closer to the edge. No railings protected anyone from the drop, which was several hundred meters down among jutting rocks, prickly shrubs, and trees. Not a fall anyone would survive without some serious injury, and not one I was anxious to experience. The woods around me seemed a sodden, gloomy world, pungent with a dark smell of soaked earth. Beyond the trail's edge, the fuzzy silhouettes of distant mountains stood against the gray sky.

Movement to the left caught my attention.

A form sprang from the trees and shoved me to the ground, the weight of a body forcing my face into the wet dirt. I decided to kick and roll, taking my attacker with me, and caught a quick glimpse of the face.

Hildick-Smith.

Interesting he'd not used his gun. Instead, he'd opted for hand-to-hand. No nerve? Or something else? An underestimation? Maybe. But enough playtime. I thrust my legs upward and recoiled his body off me, his head ending up on my belly. I shoved him off to the muddy ground, but not before driving a quick jab of my left fist into his windpipe. I sprang to my feet as he gasped, trying to find air to breathe. But I'd been careful. The force had been just enough to get his attention, but not enough to kill him.

I spat the mud from my mouth and asked, "Was all this necessary?"

He pushed himself up into a sitting position, his breathing still stabilizing. "I must . . . have . . . that box."

Which was nowhere to be seen. "Where is it?"

He motioned and I saw the knapsack propped near the trunk of a tree. "Over there."

My best option for learning what was going on seemed to be conciliatory. He was tall, gangly, maybe mid-thirties, with a thick black mat of hair, wet and not combed in any particular direction. Clearly he wasn't all that good at stealing, fleeing, or fighting. Nothing about him seemed even remotely dangerous. I stood and retrieved the knapsack, laying it on the ground beside him. Trees overhead shielded us from the majority of the rain.

"That box doesn't belong to you."

"Yes, it does."

"Not according to my friend, Nicodème."

"I tried to buy it from him. It belongs to my family. Your friend, Nicodème, bought it a few years ago in Paris at an auction house once half owned by my family. The box should have never been placed for sale. Someone did that hoping I wouldn't notice. But I did. It's how I knew your friend owned it."

"And who would do that?"

"That's what I am trying to find out." He motioned to the knapsack. "May I?"

I recalled the gun from the shop. "Where's your weapon?"

"Inside the sack."

I bent down, unzipped the top, and fished out the pistol.

"It's not loaded," he said.

I ejected the magazine and checked the chamber. No rounds anywhere.

"I just wanted to scare him," he said.

I watched as he dug into the sack and came out with a sheaf of papers, the letterhead from the Louvre in Paris. He handed them over. I shielded them from the rain and read.

> *France 16th century,* TRAVELING SABBAT CABINET WITH VARIOUS SEMI-PRECIOUS STONES SET IN GOLD BEZELS, *inscribed in pen:* 240588 - *and with illegible inscriptions to the rosewood exterior with an etched iron lock and iron handles and hinges. The interior is inlaid with ivory and marquetry in the central compartment. There are a total of 15 compartments, 10 of them containing glass bottles possibly as old as 5th century. The contents of the bottles include oils and dried herbs not as yet identified. Owner François Lussac.*

I knew the name.

The Lussac château and vineyard dated back to the 15th century. Some of the best cognac came from their label thanks to the sunshine, humidity, and the chalky reddish soil close to the marshes of southern France.

"François Lussac was my father," he said.

"I'm listening."

He seemed recovered from the assault and tossed me a semblance of a smile. "Do you have a name?"

"Cassiopeia Vitt."

"I'm Antoine Lussac," he said. "Not Peter Hildick-Smith. I thought it better to use an alias."

"Is your family related to the Lussac family who owns the château in the Cognac Valley?"

He nodded. "My older brother and I run the vineyard. Are you familiar with our brandy?"

"I am, and I'm even more familiar with the château. I've been studying medieval architecture for years."

His eyes lit. "Cassiopeia Vitt. Of course. I've read about your castle project and seen pictures. Quite an undertaking. I wish you could have met my father. He was obsessed with ancient buildings and spent a fortune restoring ours. Just like you, everything had to be original and period correct. That's how we came to own the Sabbat Box." He pointed at the knapsack. "He found it during an excavation of a cave on our property, about ten years ago."

He reached back inside and removed the box, cradling it with great care. I noticed the same inlay of stones—amethysts, moonstones, garnets, and sapphires(from when I first saw it back at the shop.

He opened the lid.

As the document from the Louvre had described, inside were compartments, each one holding a thick glass bottle dotted with bubbles and flaws. Another compartment held two small copper funnels, green with age, and another contained some uneven glass pipettes. A crisscross of wood protected each bottle, proved by the fact that during the entire run through Eze and down the mountain everything had remained intact. I examined the inside lid where a leather portfolio held bits of old paper, now decayed.

"We think there were once formulas recorded there," he said.

On the lower front were two iron pulls. I tried them, opening a drawer containing more tools. A small mortar and pestle, a knife, and an iron pan with scorch marks on its underside.

I closed the drawer. "This is extraordinary."

"It is. But don't uncork any of the bottles. Oddly, the scents are still potent. Five years ago we were doing research on them when the box disappeared. Then, as we now know, it found its way into the auction." He pointed to one. "I can attest to the fact that this bottle contains fumes with some kind of hallucinogenic properties. I experienced a wild vision when I made the mistake of taking a sniff."

Something about the box, the stones on top, the thick glass bottles, the iron corners, even the drawer, gave me pause. As if it were familiar, yet not. The feeling had started back in the shop, before the theft, while it had sat on the counter. There'd been no time to explore those feelings before all the excitement intervened.

But now—

A thought raced through my brain.

Somehow I knew that there should be vellum labels affixed to the bottom of each bottle. How? Why? I had no idea. Only that it was true. I gently touched one of them, then stopped and looked at Antoine. "May I take it out, if I don't open it?"

He nodded.

I had to see if I was right.

I lifted out the bottle. Underneath was a label. Discolored and deteriorated with age. A word, written in a sepia script, had faded but could still be read.

Belladonna.

I replaced the bottle and reached for another.

Even before I lifted it out I knew that under it would be *Diospyros*.

And I was right.

I removed a third, but before I could peek beneath it I heard the grating sound of stones being ground beneath the soles of shoes and turned to see a man leaping toward me. Antoine shoved the newcomer away, then shouted for me to grab the box and run. Before I could move, a booted foot made contact with my arm. Somehow, I kept hold of the bottle in my grasp, but I was driven down to the wet ground. I tried to recoil and go on the offensive but another blow found my brow.

Red hot pain exploded across my skull.

Then, nothing.

Chapter 3

A GREAT HALL SURROUNDS ME, ALONG WITH REVELERS INDULGING in food and wine, all celebrating the night before the last day of the new year's celebration. But I'm tired of the merriment and retire to my room.

"Are you ready for bed, my lady?" my maid asks as I enter the chamber.

"More than I can say."

I sit before the fire in the hearth and the older woman unbraids my hair, then removes my broach. I stand and I'm helped out of my heavy robes and into my night dress. Not some sack of harsh wool that peasants are forced to endure. This is silk. A shimmering red sheer. The maid withdraws to hang the dress and I climb into bed. Beside me on the nightstand sits a cup of honeyed milk. My favorite. The warm, sweet liquid always calms me.

I lie in the bed, beneath the comforter.

Sleep comes quickly.

Perhaps tonight there will be a new message.

Dreams are the Sorcerer's tool. A way of him avoiding the perils of travel, to send a message which cannot be ignored. Always, the message glows inside my head. Bright. Vibrant. Alive. With sound and smell. Even sensations. Especially the sensations. And the music. Played on a rebec and an organ, the odd combination of the stringed instrument and pipes one of the Sorceror's ways to alert my subconscious to pay attention. When the dreams first started I told myself I was a woman worthy of honor and respect. Not an old man's messenger. But I have come to welcome the visions.

Light and music appear inside my brain and I am standing by the gates to a fortress. No. The gates of my fortress. Snow falls. I feel the brisk air and the tinkle of the flakes as they dissolve on my skin. A dozen men on horseback are fast approaching. No faces are clear. Just outlines. They keep coming, riding at full gallop, but never really venture any closer.

"One of those men will one day save what is yours," the Sorcerer says to me.

His voice is its usual breathy whisper, each word perfectly enunciated.

"Save what?" I ask.

No reply.

"And from whom?"

Silence.

To find out more, I flee the gate and rush toward the horsemen, who seem to only move farther away, as does the Sorcerer's voice. He's still speaking, but I cannot hear. I call out for more explanation. There's a reply, but it echoes away like a stone down a deep well.

Which brings me awake.

My eyes open.

I shiver beneath the pelt comforter. The fire in the hearth has burned down. A chill fills the night air. What did the dream mean? I should know. I am properly schooled in the healing arts, as well as the skill of second sight. True, more Christians than Celts and Druids now exist across the kingdom, but the old ways linger. My aunt trained me as a priestess, which by its mere label makes me suspect to all those who have adopted the one god philosophy of Christ. Priestesses are now called witches, as people fear what they do not understand.

Particularly men.

No. Just weak men.

Jealous of the power women possess. A power a man can never have. The ability to give life. And that, coupled with lust and passion, can become a threat. Women are never perceived as dangerous because they might rebel or conspire. But dare to control a man? To have him do what he might not ever normally do?

That is a power men fear.

Men long for us. Yearn for us. They grow stupid wanting us. A smart woman can exploit that weakness. I have done so many times and will do it again. But in retaliation for their own shortcomings, their own mistakes, weak men have come to label intelligent women witches.

But there is no such thing.

The late hour, the crackle of the dying fire and the effects from the honeyed milk once again make my eyes heavy.

Sleep is returning.

Which I welcome, knowing the messages are over for the night.

I awake.

Morning has arrived.

I rise from the bed and send my maid to retrieve a bowl of rain water, wine, and oil. I'm still bothered by not being able to hear all of the Sorcerer's message. I should have stayed by the gate and listened to what he had to say. The dream had felt portentous, and I need to try and glimpse the future and perhaps learn what the Sorcerer was trying to tell me.

The maid returns with the rainwater in a wooden bowl. I drop in oil until the surface is glassy and reflective. I send her away and strip down naked. To the fire in the hearth I offer sage leaves and juniper berries, savoring their scents in the chilly air, staring into the oily surface, trancelike. It takes a moment, but an image appears. A man, unknown to me, and the Sorcerer, talking to one another. The other man gestures and a beam of light shoots from the ring he is wearing. A thick band of gold, with a red stone at its center, that glows like the sun.

"You shall know from the color of the stone," the Sorcerer whispers from the surface of the water.

Then his voice grows faint. I bend close to hear more. His mouth moves but I cannot determine his words.

"Say it again," I tell the image.

But he is gone.

A sense of anticipation rolls through me, followed by joy, then dread.

None of which I understand.

I don my favorite robe, purple shot through with red silken threads, then have my maid weave a red ribbon into my long dark hair. I fasten my mother's moonstone necklace about my thin neck and hasten to join the late-morning festivities outside of the castle walls. The fifteen-day celebration of the new year is drawing to a close with a final tournament. I take my place of honor in the crowd, doing what is expected from Arturius' sister, though if only half by blood. As leader he is likewise in attendance and acknowledges me with a casual wave and a smile.

"My lady?"

The voice comes from behind me and I turn to face a man.

He's handsome with black hair, firm jaw, and deep, almost liquid eyes. I do not know him so I say only, "How may I help?"

"I'm Helians of Gormet."

And he holds out his hand.

On one finger I see a heavy gold ring, its stone flashing the red color of the silk in my dress.

You shall know from the color of the stone.

From the Sorcerer.

My senses come instantly alert but my face and eyes betray nothing. The mask, I call it. Essential for survival in a man's world.

"Might I wear your colors in the fight?" he asks me with a smile.

It's not an unusual request, as it is customary for the participants to seek a female patron. Why I was chosen remains a mystery. But the ring he wears signals the correct reply.

"I would be honored, good sir."

Over the next hour I watch as Helians bests all competitors. No one rises to the challenge, and every time he catches my eye I feel my cheeks flush, my blood warming. A strange and different sensation, but one I welcome. Particularly since I was warned that this man might prove important. No break occurs before the evening festivities, so I'm not able to speak with him. But I find myself spending more time preparing my hair and clothes, in anticipation of seeing him at the late meal.

I arrive as the men enter the great hall after attending Mass, singing shouts of Noel, Noel. Bright torches illuminate the cavernous space. Tapestries hang from the walls and trap the warmth from two hearths that burn bright. Smells dominate. So many, mingling together like sweat on skin. Roasted meat. Baking bread. Sweet oils the men and women wear. Many people of high standing fill the tables, drinking and eating with abandon. The merrymaking continues for hours, the mood growing more and more carefree as more wine is consumed. Whether by chance, or at his specific request, or thanks to Arturius' insight—I do not know which— Helians has been seated beside me. Our talks are interesting. His travels. My family. Our fortresses. The longer he keeps me at arm's length, the more outrageous my flirtations become.

Coy has never been my nature.

My aunt taught me the ways of the old world. I live by an uncommon belief system. *Always have. Always will. Which can lead to trouble. But knowing that the meek inherit nothing, I lean forward and lay a hand on his arm, making sure he notices my décolletage. Tomorrow I head back home. This may be my only opportunity to understand the Sorcerer's message.*

"Good sister," Arturius calls out from across the hall. "Will you honor us with a song?"

The moment between us breaks.

I turn and catch my half-brother's eye and nod, knowing that the request must be granted. I enjoy showing off my voice and the performance is well received. After finishing three songs, while accepting the compliments of those present, Helians offers his personal praise and presents me with a gift, a token of good luck, he says, for the coming months.

"It's the finest thing I have brought with me and I'm pleased to offer it to the finest maiden here."

He opens his fist and reveals the gold ring studded with a ruby.

"Place it on my finger, please," I say. "So that I may always think of your hand touching mine."

If he is shocked by my forwardness he hides his surprise. But my message is clearly heard for once the ring is on my finger, he draws me with him into a carola, *joining hands with the other dancers. His eager glances to my lips and breasts, and my encouraging smiles of agreement inflames us both.*

He wants me.

Once the song ends we slip from the great hall and hurry toward my room.

The next few hours change my life.

Had he not pursued me. Had I not responded. Had we not begun our lovemaking in the hallway before retiring to my bedchamber. Had he not been such an ardent lover. Had I not been so anxious to understand the message.

So much would be different.

Chapter 4

I OPENED MY EYES AND LOOKED AROUND EXPECTING TO BE INSIDE A great hall lit by torches. To see trestle tables lined with men and women making New Year's merry. Instead I was lying on the wet ground, my right cheek in the mud, staring out at a rugged mountainside and the azure sea made hazy by rain. The glass bottle from the box, the one I'd been examining right before the attack, lay at an angle beneath me, its stopper partly uncorked. I righted the bottle and plugged it, making sure the top was tight, remembering Antoine's warning about smelling what was inside.

The vision had been so vivid. Like a curtain within my mind had parted. As if I were there. Somewhere else. In another time.

Then I recalled the attack.

A few deep breaths cleared my lungs. My brow ached, the pain even more intense than my bruised feet. Whoever attacked me must have hit my head, with a boot, if I wasn't mistaken. The world spun, like being drunk off far too much wine without the pleasure of ingesting it.

I blinked the cobwebs away from my eyes.

Antoine lay on the ground beside me. Unconscious with a nasty gash to the side of his head. Blood oozed from the wound and had congealed in his hair. I crawled over and felt his pulse. Slow and weak. His breathing seemed labored too. He needed a hospital. The nearest one was in Nice about a dozen kilometers away. I reached for my cell phone but it was gone. Had it fallen out? I looked around. Nothing. It was with me when I left the shop. I searched Antoine's pockets hoping he had a phone. Nothing. The backpack and the wooden box had also vanished. All I had was the one vial that had gone down with me.

I glanced at my watch.

4:08 p.m.

Two hours had passed since the attack.

That shocked me.

Two hours we'd lain here in the rain and no one had come by?

I tried to wake Antoine, but he would not rouse. No way I could carry him back up to the village or down to ground level. I had no choice but to head for help. I pocketed the vial, then stood, fighting the dizziness, my legs trembling. I moved as fast as I could back up to town. Fifteen minutes later I banged the iron hand knocker on the door to the shop.

Nicodème answered.

"Cassiopeia. Finally. I've been so worried about you." He stared at my bedraggled appearance. "Are you all right? What happened?"

"I'm not hurt badly, but telling you about that has to wait. There's someone who is unconscious and injured."

I described Antoine's injuries and where I'd left him, then said, "He's the thief."

Nicodème immediately made a phone call to the local emergency service and in rapid French described the situation and the victim's location.

"The medics will be sent," he said, as he hung up. "Now what about you?"

I was barefoot, soaking wet, and muddy. My clothes clung to me like a soaked towel. "I need to get back to him."

"Are you capable?" he asked.

"My feet are sore. My head hurts. And I have a bump the size of an egg, but I'll live."

I didn't mention the glass vial in my pocket. Not yet, anyway. A little voice in my head told me to hold that knowledge for now. I gingerly touched the top of my head and grimaced. That bastard's boot caught me hard.

"Are you okay?" he asked.

"I'll be fine. But if you have them, I'll take two pain killers."

He shuffled across the shop to a bathroom, opened a cabinet, and found a couple of pills which I swallowed without water.

"Can you tell me exactly what happened?" he asked.

"I'll tell you everything, but I need to go back and make sure they come for Antoine."

Then I realized he didn't know.

"Peter Hildick-Smith was an alias."

The revelation didn't appear to shock him. "I'll come with you. You're in no state to handle things alone."

I shook my head. "Someone dangerous is out there and I don't want to worry about you too. I'll be back as soon as the medics take him."

I stared down at my feet. I needed shoes. "You don't happen to have a pair I could wear, do you?"

"Sylvie's still got some clothes here," he said referring to his daughter who lived just down the hill in Nice. She was married, with two children. She and her husband owned a wonderful restaurant by the sea I'd frequented often.

"That might work," I said.

He left and returned with a pair of espadrilles a minute later. "These are all that was there."

He handed them to me.

"They'll work," I said, wincing as I forced my feet into them. At least they were a half size bigger or I never would have been able to wear them. My soles screamed in pain, but there was no time to give in to the discomfort. "I'll come back as soon—"

"Do you have a phone?"

"It's gone."

He disappeared for a few seconds, returning with a phone. "Take mine. Call on my landline, if you need me."

I pocketed the cell and left the shop, following the same route I'd taken before, winding through the cobbled streets to the viewing platform, then climbing over the railing. The rain had eased to more of a drizzle. Luckily the day was unseasonably warm, the air comfortable even with the wet. I reached the area where I'd twice been ambushed. Antoine was gone. Had the medics already arrived and taken him off? If so, that had been fast. Had someone else come along and helped him down the trail? I found the phone and called Nicodème, explaining what I'd discovered and asked him to check with the local hospital and find out if they had him. He told me he'd be back to me shortly.

I stood there and surveyed the scene. What a day. My clothes were ruined, including an expensive silk Armani shirt and a pair of Louis Vuitton shoes. I'd dressed to meet Nicodème for lunch, not chase a man through the rain and fight in the mud. I still had the one bottle from the Sabbat Box in my pocket, which I slipped out and examined. On its bottom, on a faded parchment label was the word *Henbane*.

What it meant I had no idea.

The dream in the great hall, then at the banquet lingered in my mind. I'd never experienced anything like that before. What had Antoine said? *The fumes have some kind of hallucinogenic properties. I experienced a wild vision when I made the mistake of taking a sniff.* Was there a corollary between the bottle and vision?

One way to find out.

I sat against an out-of-the-way tree in case my theory proved correct. I popped the cork free and brought the bottle to my nose. The scent seemed unusually fresh and sweet. Was it orange? Or lime? Hard to tell.

I recorked the bottle.

Then I saw trees.

And—

The forest looms heavy with rain.

A canopy of leaves provides some shelter, but I do not stop to seek protection. I love rain. It cleanses me. Makes me feel connected with both the earth and the sky, like nature's release, as pleasurable and spontaneous as the joy between a man and a woman.

I tighten the reins and drive my mare at a trot through the dripping branches. My hair and cloak are soaked. But it's necessary. I've come to gather plants needed for my box. I do not like for its contents to draw low. Nothing can be mixed without the proper ingredients and, sometimes, to gather those, it's necessary to get wet. The day is fading and I must hurry back and prepare for the evening.

A visitor is on the way.

Sir Helians.

Four weeks have passed since we last lay together.

He is extraordinary in so many ways, and the thought of welcoming him back to my bed, along with the rhythmic movement from the horse's gallop, sends waves of pleasure up through me, reminding me of what I've been missing.

I see a horse approaching from ahead. I slow and spot my servant. He yanks his reins, stopping before me.

"There's trouble up ahead, mistress," Erec says. "A dozen men are waiting for you at the fortress gates, and none are from Sir Helians' party."

I'm alarmed. But the harassment is not unexpected. Six factors have long been working against me. I'm only Arturius' half-sister. I was also once his lover, though we did not know of our relation at the time. I gave birth to his son. His wife hates me. Many have labeled me a witch. And witch hunts are growing in popularity.

"Ride ahead," I tell Erec, "and tell my lady to ready the oils and unguents, then find two empty jars. Bring my Sabbat Box and the jars to the road that winds around the back of the fortress, where they'll not be expecting me."

He nods and rides away at a fast pace. He's a good servant, in my charge for many years. Utterly trustworthy.

Or as trustworthy as anyone could be.

By the time I reach the place of assignation, Erec is there with my box at the ready. I dismount and open it with the key I wear on a chain around my neck. Inside are bottles of dried herbs, leaves, barks, flowers, and oils that, when mixed properly, accomplish feats that, to the uninformed, appear to be magic. But they are simply the power of plants. Chymistry, the Sorcerer would say. The natural result when differing substances combine and change into something new. The skill comes from knowing how to combine them.

A skill I've mastered.

I know of many compounds. Some help the sick. A few inflame men. Others give women relief during childbirth or rid them of an unwanted pregnancy. A few open a portal to the past or allow me to gleam the future. The power of the plants seems boundless. But also frightening. Some people claim I'm a shapeshifter, a seductress, a monster, a wonder, sometimes even a ghost. One term has come to sum up all of their accusations into a single indictment.

Witch.

I learned about plants from the Sorcerer. He showed me how to find them in the woods, how to dry and prepare them, how to mix them in the right amounts. The one I now combine will make the men awaiting me grow tired and sleep, which will allow me the opportunity to re-enter the safety of the fortress without incident.

I know why these men have come.

But Sir Helians will arrive soon and I must be ready.

I slip my horse's dry caparison from the saddle bag and lay it on the *wet ground under a giant oak. From my box I measure out the needed herbs and oils. I pour some of the mixture into one jar, the rest into the other.*

When I finish, I face Erec. "Walk stealthily around to where the horsemen wait. Stay upwind. Once you are close enough to smell them, combine the liquids into one jar. I've also prepared this soaked cloth for you to breathe through, so you will not be affected. Even so, be careful. Once you've set the jar down, move away to a spot where you can watch without inhaling the fouled air. The wind will carry it their way. After they've succumbed and are asleep, come back to me."

"Is it a spell?" Erec asks.

I smile, knowing that is what the uneducated call my mixtures. "Not at all. It's a blessed balm. It works wonderfully on children to help them sleep, or on soldiers suffering from wounds to give them relief. But not for women with child because it can cause trouble with the babes."

"Do you know who these strangers may be?" he asks.

"They come in another attempt to take my home. Sent by my loving half-brother, and his angry, deceitful wife. Go now, and do as I say."

In less than an hour Erec returns, slightly out of breath. "All are fast asleep."

I mount my horse and we circle to the front, past the sleeping armed men, and across the drawbridge to the gates, which are opened for my return.

Another onslaught averted.

But it will not be the last.

Chapter 5

I SLIPPED OUT OF THE HALLUCINATION, SURPRISED ONCE AGAIN BY both the journey and the return. The forest and the fortress had seemed so real. So had Erec. And the potion, and the sleeping armed men. I checked my watch. I'd been out about a half hour.

I found the phone and saw that Nicodème had not called. I lay on the wet ground, the corked bottle beside me. The rain had ended, but the storm still lingered out over the sea. I stared at the footpath. What was it? A ninety-minute walk down to the water. Antoine and I had traversed less than a quarter of it before we'd been ambushed. If medics had driven up to Eze, then walked down to find him I would have passed them. If they'd walked up from the bottom of the path they wouldn't have even arrived yet.

So where did Antoine go?

I thought about Nietzsche walking the footpath, planning a book that later became misconstrued, co-opted by Nazis who exploited and twisted his message. I'd read it and saw it for what it was, a meditation on the dangers of becoming overzealous about religion. I imagined that some who walked this path thought on the philosopher's belief in a free, passionate, chaotic life-force. One unchecked by man or rules. I wondered how many of them experienced dreams so vivid they seemed real? I'd never spent much time focused on the occult but, as I sat there, staring at where Antoine had lain, looking at the glass bottle with god-knows what inside, I wondered what was happening.

The phone hummed.

Nicodème.

"The hospital says the medics are on the way," he told me.

So Antoine either got up and walked away or someone helped him.

"I need to find where he is," I said.

"Why don't you come back here and we can—"

"I don't want to wait. The more time that passes the colder the trail gets."

At least that's what experience had taught me.

"What are you going to do?"

"I'll walk down to make sure he didn't pass out along the path. If I don't find him, I'll take my car and head to the hospital, then ring you."

And that was what I did, seeing nothing of Antoine. Two hours later, I reached the hospital in Nice. He wasn't in the waiting room, had not been admitted, nor was there anyone there matching his description. By the time I returned to Eze it was almost eight p.m. My feet and body ached and the sun was setting.

"Maybe his wound wasn't as serious as you thought," Nicodème said as he filled a glass with water. "For now, I want you to sit. You need to have something to eat and drink."

"I need a bath and change of clothes."

He chuckled. "That you do."

"I'd also love some wine."

"First, water," he said, with a fatherly concern.

While I drank, he arranged a platter with cheese, olives, and a slab of pâté. He sliced a fresh baguette and tossed the bread in a wicker basket. After setting the food on the table he added plates, silverware, napkins, a pitcher of water, and finally a bottle of rosé. I reached for the wine and poured us both a glass. We ate and he questioned me in detail. I recapped the whole series of events, everything that had happened from the time I'd run from the shop chasing the thief. The only thing I omitted was the glass bottle in my pocket and the two visions. I'm not sure why I didn't confess those too, but I'd learned to trust my instincts.

And they told me to keep silent.

"Antoine said the box belonged to his family. Is that right?"

"I have no idea. I bought it at auction years ago, as he told you."

"What exactly is it?"

"Supposedly when witches and sorcerers gathered for rites, dancing, or feasting they brought with them their individual herbs and potions, all carried in a Sabbat Box. Usually plain wood with some carvings, this one was more elegant, which may have signaled that its original owner was a person of means."

Like a leader's half-sister, I thought to myself.

"Some of the bottles contain herbal extracts," he said. "Others flower and oils. Some are identified, others are not."

I recalled the three labels.

Belladonna. Diospyros. Henbane.

"The legend associated with this Sabbat Box suggests that, among those bottles, were three particular potions of note. My cousin, Jac L'Etoile, who runs the family perfume company, performed some chemical analysis on samples from some of the bottles. Ones that supposedly have some applicability to reincarnation. That's what drew my interest."

I was intrigued. "What do you mean?"

"Since ancient times, mystics and shamans have believed that the door to our past life memories lies in deep meditation. Over the centuries there have been a dozen or so memory tools that have become aids in reaching that state. Psychologists use hypnosis to achieve the same result, especially in patients whose phobias or psychoses defy other treatment. Past life memories can many times explain present day issues. A proven method that allows us to reach into past life memories would be invaluable. Think of the demand. Think of the wisdom, the lost knowledge, the treasures, the solutions to so many mysteries that could be recovered if such an aid to the past actually existed. A few years ago, a rumor surfaced that a perfume had been discovered that was just such a memory tool. My cousin, Robbie L'Etoile, was almost killed for it. My hope was that this Sabbat Box may contain another version of that same compound."

"So when you heard it was for sale, you bought it?"

He nodded. "Then I immediately sent samples to Jac, in Paris, to see if the two formulas match."

"According to Antoine, the box you bought at auction was not supposed to go on sale. It was put up by mistake. He was trying to reclaim his family's heritage. And apparently so was someone else."

"The auction house never provided me the name of the box's owner, but I knew François Lussac was part owner in Du Lac Auctions. That's where I bought the box. How is it possible his own items were sold there by mistake?"

"Antoine didn't know."

Nicodème stood and walked over to his bar, returning with a decanter of caramel-colored liquid.

"That family's cognac is some of the finest."

He poured us both a splash. "Do you believe what Antoine told you?"

"I didn't at first, but now I'm not so sure."

"There's not much we can do," he said. "The box is gone. The thief is gone. But I'm worried, Cassiopeia. What if the person who's taken the box tries to use the oils, not realizing they could be toxic?"

Something told me that the second thief knew more about the Sabbat Box than anyone. But I decided to humor my old friend. "That's certainly a possibility."

"It's old and of some historical interest, and its connections to the aesthetic and arcane are fascinating. I want it back. Can you help me find it?"

I'd like nothing better.

For a half hour, we tossed around ideas. I also made a call to my château and asked for someone to bring me some shoes and clothes, providing a list so a bag could be packed. The time was approaching 9 p.m., but I decided to make a second call.

To Harold Earl "Cotton" Malone.

The love of my life.

I was supposed to check in with him two hours ago. He'd probably already tried my cell phone, but who knows where that was now. We'd been together a few years, our initial meeting anything but pleasant. It had taken time and tribulations for us to become a couple, our relationship sometimes as rocky as the Philosopher's Walk. But there was no one I trusted, or admired, more. No one I'd rather spend my time with.

Or ask for advice.

As a former Justice Department operative, Cotton was smart and capable. Fearless too. And, luckily, the same things seemed to fascinate us.

Action, history, secrets, and conspiracies.

I borrowed Nicodème's phone and used FaceTime to connect. Cotton had retired out early and now lived in Copenhagen, about to leave tomorrow for the United States to visit his son. It was good to see his handsome face.

I explained my day.

"I'm not sure I should go now," he said, concern in his tone.

"I'm fine. I'm going to stay and find out what's going on." I pointed the phone's camera at Nicodème. "Tell him I'm okay."

The two men knew one another, having met over a year ago, sharing an interest in books. Cotton owned a rare bookshop in Denmark and Nicodème had several times helped him acquire some collectible volumes.

"I have my eye on her," Nicodème said. "She'll be okay."

I smiled at the fatherly tone. But I realized that the fact that my new protector was approaching eighty wasn't lost on my all-too-practical boyfriend.

"Humor me," Cotton said. "Explain exactly what happened again. Even if you think you're repeating yourself. Step by step. Something in this story doesn't add up."

I had to be careful with what I withheld and how, since I knew he could read me. Keeping part of the story from him wasn't something I liked doing, and we'd both learned our lesson on withholding secrets from one another. But I was still processing the dreams myself and didn't, as yet, know how to explain them. Instead, I stuck to the string of events themselves and joined Nicodème in recounting the story. Several times he stopped us to go over a point, then we kept going. I saw on the screen where he was typing on a keyboard.

"It seems the Lussac family is influential in French politics," he pointed out. "Antoine is one of three brothers. Emile and Antoine run the vineyard. Denton is a French political operative who's worked for various people. He's got quite the reputation, and not all good. Here's something interesting. Antoine and Emile have publicly denounced Denton for some of his more egregious scandals. There are several online articles that deal with the brothers. Denton is quite the character. Doesn't seem to have many scruples. He does what he needs to do to win an election. But he gets results. Tell me about the bidding at the auction house."

Nicodème recounted the story, adding, "One of the issues with the Sabbat Box was that it was mismarked, dated only to the early 1800s in the catalog. That affected the price, to say the least. I knew better. Thankfully, that day's sale was all mediocre objects from the Belle Époque that attracted almost no attention. I had few people bidding against me."

I stepped into the other room with the phone to say goodbye in private.

"You take care of yourself," Cotton said, his eyes seeming to connect with mine.

"I could say the same to you."

"I'm just going to visit Gary."

"And I'm just here with an old friend checking on a few things."

Neither one of us was overly sentimental, but we both knew how the other felt.

"I love you," he said.

I softened my voice, allowing myself the moment to miss him. "I love you too."

He winked before ending the call.

I refocused my thoughts, stepping back into the shop to find Nicodème flipping through a booklet. "What's that?"

"The catalog from the sale of the Sabbat Box. I need to call Claude Mantte."

I didn't know the name.

"He's the manager of the auction house."

"But it's after nine-thirty at night."

"Claude is a friend, and I spend a lot of money with him. He won't mind."

While Nicodème talked on the shop's landline I used his computer to check my emails. Quite a few had piled up while I'd been occupied. The only ones I answered were from the foreman at my building site. As I was finishing up, a new one appeared from Cotton.

Look at this. I knew that Denton Lussac sounded familiar.

Cotton possessed an eidetic memory, which often came in handy. It also allowed him to never forget a word I ever said, which rarely led to anything good. I was about to click on the link he'd provided when Nicodème hung up the phone and said, "Something is really strange about this."

I waited for him to explain.

"That Sabbat Box was indeed sold by mistake. Two people called the day of the sale, both claiming to be the owner. One was Denton Lussac. The other Antoine Lussac. Separately, both brothers claimed the box should have been removed because it was part of their father's estate. But Claude just told me that the late Monsieur Lussac had brought the box in himself, over six months before he died, with instructions to sell it after his death. Both of the brothers were quite upset. Denton even threatened litigation. Which Claude was not worried about, considering the sale was legitimate. He just asked me, though, if I'd be willing to allow the brothers to buy it back from me.

At a premium."

"I know what you said to that."

"As I told our thief, it belongs in the museum and that's where I intend to keep it. Once you get it back, of course."

"Did Claude provide the brothers your name? Is that how Antoine found you?"

Nicodème nodded. "Only recently. But here's the strangest part, what I did not tell Claude. Before he died Monsieur Lussac himself wrote me, told me about the box, and that it would be for sale soon. He suggested it was something I might want to own. I wrote back and said I would look into it and asked why he thought I might want it. But he never answered that inquiry."

I was puzzled. "Why would Monsieur Lussac not just give you the box? Why go through an auction?"

He shook his head. "I have no idea."

He stood and told me he was going to make tea and asked if I wanted some. I said I did. He left the room. I remembered the link Cotton had sent and clicked on it. It took me to a French news site featuring an article about the unpopular president of France, Yves Casimir, who was running against a strong challenger, Lydia St. Benedict. Most of it was unimportant information but toward the end of the article, there was a mention of Lydia St. Benedict's staff, including her most trusted associates.

And I saw it.

There, among the names.

Denton Lussac.

I prepared for bed.

I'd stayed over before with Nicodème and loved the attic room. With the window open, a breeze easing in, nestled in the canopied bed, I always felt like I was sleeping in the sky. The room had been his daughter's, still filled with a young woman's books and accessories. A mini-shrine of sorts that I was sure Nicodème enjoyed preserving. I also loved the lemony scent, the result of a verbena and melissa oil diffuser.

I stepped out of my filthy jeans and ruined shirt. The room came with a small bath which I used to clean up. I was promised a bag of clean clothes and shoes first thing in the morning, so I decided to sleep naked tonight.

The glass bottle sat on the dresser, its stopper down tight. I brought it over to the nightstand and sat on the side of the bed, wrapped in a towel. Nicodème had warned me about the possible effects from the concoctions in the box, as had Antoine. But for some reason I wasn't concerned. Nor was I frightened of the hallucinations. If that was what they were. In fact, I wanted more. Was that an addiction? Possibly.

But I couldn't resist.

I removed the stopper.

And sniffed.

Then quickly re-corked the top.

Chapter 6

I SMILE.

Erec tells me that a message has arrived. Sir Helians is less than an hour away.

The men outside at the gates had awoken from their sleep, terrified, unsure what happened to them. They'd fled their post, riding off into the forest. I watched their retreat with relief. Now I'm filled with joy and I hurry to the kitchen to check on the preparations for the evening meal. All seems ready, so I retire to my bedchamber for the most important preparations.

My lover is coming for what promises to be a fulfilling sojourn. It is important that he crave me. Want me. Even more important, he must be proud of himself once his desires are satisfied. That pride will ensure his continued protection of my home. I have a great knowledge of chymistry, an understanding of the natural world, but I do not possess an army of soldiers. And sometimes men with swords are needed.

"Draw a bath," I tell my maid, "and sprinkle in rose petals. I'll also need the cream I prepared earlier, for after the bath."

My trip into the rain proved productive. I found the plants I was seeking. While the men slept outside the gates I had prepared the salve. Made special for my inner thighs, under my breasts, and behind my ears. All places Helians would surely explore.

He will like the effects.

As will I.

Helians arrives at the castle with a wound to his shin from an unexpected skirmish on the journey. I lead him to my workshop where I clean the flesh, then apply a healing salve. He winces at its properties, which burn, but *that only means it's working. I apply a bandage and he grabs me around the waist, sitting me on his lap. I inhale his scent of fire and smoke mixed with the waft of apples and pine.*

He laughs. "I do love how you always take a sniff of me when first we meet again."

"So many men stink." I point to his chest. "You do not."

"It's the potion you made. I spread it on my skin, under my arms, and it keeps all the bad odors away. Only attracts the good ones."

I smile. "Just the way I like it."

He nuzzles close to my neck and breathes in my scent, laced with the fragrant cream I applied after my bath. "You smell of secrets and velvet and the sea. And roses. Always roses."

He kisses my lips and I kiss him back, glad the long month of missing him is over. His fingertips are a little rough and, as he runs them down my neck, I shiver at the excitement from the sensation. Of all the men I've known, this one knows the art of touch the best.

"I've missed you," he whispers.

He opens the laces at the front of my gown, parting the folds, not taking quite as much time as I would have liked. But I share his haste. I want to feel his arms across my bare back, my breasts pressed against him. I want to rake my fingers through the hair on his chest.

I want him.

He bends and gifts kisses down my neck. His tongue paints a trail of want to the pale skin of my belly. My excitement makes me smile. He lifts his head from my breast and I stare deep at his winsome face, smiling back. Oh, how he pleases me. As a priestess I'm betrothed to no man. I possess the freedom to take pleasure with anyone.

And I have chosen Helians.

I run my fingers through his rough and tumble hair, down his forehead, across his jutting cheekbones and along the bump in his nose. His eyes are heavy with passion and something else. Something troubling. I see his pain. Pictures form in my mind, but I push them away.

Not now.

I stand from his lap and remove his shirt, then bend over and kiss his cheek, burying my face in his skin and savoring more of his scent. Of all my lovers, Helians has lasted the longest. Some of that is from simple attraction. Some is from herbs and oils that strengthen his desire. Aphrodisiacs have proven worthwhile additions to my pharmacy.

"What say we move to your bed." His voice is hoarse with need. "I've

been traveling for many days and nights and lying down would be welcome."

I take him by the hand and lead him to my bedchamber. No servants are around. All have been told to stay away unless summoned. My bed awaits us both, a gift from Arturius when we were still on the best of terms. I undress him and he lies down naked. I love the time between wanting and taking. To see how much I'm desired, while feeling my own desires build. He watches me, his mouth slightly open, his body tense and taut. I bend over him and run a finger from his shoulder, down the center of his chest, past his navel, then across one thigh to a knee to a calf to ankle to foot, then up from the other foot following the same exact path in reverse until I reach his lips. He opens his mouth, grips my finger between his teeth, and gives me a playful bite.

I withdraw my finger.

"I'll bite harder if you don't let me take the rest of those clothes off of you. I can't bear much more of this waiting."

I slowly finish undressing. He reaches out to pull me closer, but I step back, out of reach, playing our game. Desire, at its best, must be painful for both. The greater the pain, the more powerful the pleasure will be.

"Enough. Come here now," he finally says.

He pulls me on top of him, wrapping his arms around me, kissing me hard on the lips. I want to dissolve into him with no more waiting.

His entrance comes with ease.

I meet each of his thrusts with one of my own, a familiar dance we've enjoyed before. Failed efforts to slow down, and spread it out, reveal the time we've been apart.

But we both try.

"Not yet," I beg, murmuring into his ear.

I keep riding him without any pretense of maidenly modesty. I no longer care how much he knows I want him. We are beyond that now. His life as a warrior is fraught with danger. Every time he leaves my bed I'm never sure if I will see him again.

And that fear fuels our passion.

"I'm trying to hold on, woman, but you're an evil temptress."

It never bothers me when he calls me that. I trust him and know he does not fear my power. Instead, he savors it, craves it, wants it.

He reaches the end.

Deep inside of me his final thrusts silence all thought and fill me with a pleasure so intense it is only a feather's distance away from pain. He lets out a long moan that lingers and I savor the sound of his release as he bucks up and plunges deeper to my center, where molten fires burn and sparks escape into my blood, causing every piece of me to feel like a burst of flames. We lie there, spent, breathing heavy, wet with each other's perspiration, exhausted, luxuriating in the magic we've made. I do not say a word and do not expect him to speak either.

But he does.

"Arturius is determined to have this fortress back."

I am about to reply, but he places a finger to my lips.

"I know. He gave it to you. But his wife has made him hate you. Her jealousy over your giving him a son, and her not being able to give him a child at all, has turned her against you with a fury that knows no bounds. She demands that you be banished. He has refused. But, to appease her, he has promised to send his best men to reclaim this site."

"Men came today."

"I met them on the way here. It is they who I fought."

My heart fills with gratitude.

"But they will not be the last who come," he says. "Morgan le Fay, you are a marked woman."

I do not like those words. But they're true.

"Even worse, the man placed in charge of the effort to evict you is one of your former lovers."

I grimace and know who it must be. "Your brother?"

He nods. "Whom I must oppose."

The cruelty of Arturius is clear, the irony not lost.

Kaz of Gormet versus Helians of Gormet.

One brother to attack my home, the other to defend it.

Chapter 7

I AWOKE WITH A START. SUNLIGHT GLEAMED BEYOND THE OPEN window. Morning had arrived. Had I fallen asleep during the hallucination? Apparently so, since my towel still hung lose around my body. And what a sleep. Again, the dream had seemed so real. As if I were there, experiencing what she was experiencing. Even the sex. As if I were there. Which was unsettling, to say the least.

I sat up on the side of the bed and allowed my head to clear. Like the two times before the images faded fast, lingering only a few moments, like smoke from a fire. Their fleetingness made me question their reality. But there was no denying that the potion in that glass bottle had power.

And now two names were stuck in my head.

Sir Helians of Gormet and Morgan le Fay.

I forced my mind to calm.

Last night I'd brought Nicodème's laptop upstairs with me. I reached for the machine and opened to a search engine, typing in the two names.

Morgan le Fay possessed an uncertain past, most likely from Welsh mythology, a Celtic goddess figure. She rose to fame as the invention of Sir Thomas Malory in his *Le Morte d'Arthur* as one of the half-sisters of King Arthur. An apprentice to Merlin and a redoubtable adversary to the Knights of the Round Table, she was fiercely independent and sexually voracious. She became Queen Guinevere's lady in waiting and fell in love with Arthur's nephew. Guinevere put an end to the romance and, as a result, she eventually betrayed the queen's affair with Lancelot to Arthur. Overall, she seemed a fairly wicked, conniving character with few redeeming social values, her personality darkening each time the Arthurian legend was retold. She was usually cast as a healer, villain, enchantress, seductress, or a combination thereof. In modern times feminists had adopted her as a symbol of power, choosing to cast her as a benevolent figure with extraordinary abilities.

Helians of Gormet seemed much more mysterious, with little to nothing noted about him except that the various poets who retold the Arthurian legend liked to cast him as one of Morgan's countless lovers.

What in the world was happening?

Never had I read *Le Morte d'Arthur* or any of its many variations. Clearly Morgan le Fay wasn't real. Just part of a legend. Of course, the debate had raged for centuries. Had Malory simply made the entire tale up? Every detail in his story fiction? Or had he adapted actual stories that had existed for years prior to the mid-15th century, when his book first appeared?

Nobody knew.

I showered and found an overnight bag waiting outside the door. Thank goodness. My people had come through. I dressed and located Nicodème downstairs in the kitchen. Over coffee and fresh croissants from the local baker, he told me he'd checked with the hospital but no one matching Antoine's description had ever been admitted.

Which was troubling.

We explored the various possibilities but got nowhere. His disappointment at losing the Sabbat Box seemed almost as great as his concern over Antoine's disappearance.

"Are you still willing to track down both the box and Antoine?" he asked.

I nodded.

But first it was time to come clean.

I told him about the glass bottle and the three visions.

"Why didn't you tell me this yesterday?" he asked.

"I'm not sure. Maybe I wanted to explore them further first. Now I know. They weren't dreams. I wasn't an observer. I was there, as someone else."

He smiled. "Not someone else, Cassiopeia. They were past life memories. Your memories, released. That bottle does exactly what the legends claim. It opens a door in your mind."

Which was hard for me to accept since I don't believe in reincarnation.

"You do realize," he said, "that your fascination with medieval times and your desire to rebuild a castle stems from a past life experience."

I'd never considered that possibility. But I'd also never quite understood my obsession with the project either. Especially considering the millions of euros it cost.

"I want to know more about that formula," I said. "I want to know if and how it's causing those hallucinations."

"Then that's where you should start. Go and see my cousin in Paris and ask her what she discovered. She can explain it far better than I. But I can call Claude at the auction house and have him meet with you too."

"And the glass bottle?"

"Take it with you."

I climbed the stairs back to my room and gathered my things. When I descended, ready to go, Nicodème met me at the door with a brown paper bag. "A baguette with Camembert and ham. For the train ride from Nice to Paris."

I smiled, appreciative of his efforts.

"Stay safe," he told me.

It was seven p.m. when I arrived in Paris.

The Montalembert was a boutique hotel on the Left Bank housed in a lovely 1926 building, just off St. Germain des Prés. I often stayed there not only for its old-world ambiance, but modern functionality. I texted Cotton from Nicodème's phone to let him know how to find me, but he didn't answer. After a light supper from room service, I watched an old black and white movie and was about to go to sleep when a gentle beep interrupted the silence. Cotton replying? I read the phone's screen alert and was shocked.

Called the shop and Nicodème provided this number. I'm in Paris. Antoine.

I replied and told him we should meet.

Not yet. Soon.

I debated what to do, but decided I had no choice. He was calling the shots. I glanced at the stoppered bottle lying on the dresser, debating whether to again allow an intrusion.

No. Not tonight.

So I slept.

Without dreaming.

Chapter 8

I LEFT THE HOTEL EARLY, THE BRIGHT PARISIAN MORNING WARM, AND headed toward the Seine. My hotel sat only three blocks away from my appointment with Jac L'Etoile.

Rue des Saints-Pères was a narrow street lined with residences and antique shops. Nestled between two of them I found my destination and rang its doorbell. A returning buzz sounded which released an electronic lock. I turned the knob and entered L'Etoile Parfums, one of Paris' most iconic perfume shops, dating back to before the French Revolution.

A bouquet of scents greeted my nose, as did the period decor. Mottled antique mirrors covered the walls and ceiling, scattered atop murals of pastel flowers and angels. My attention was drawn to the rosewood cabinets against two walls, each filled with antique perfume paraphernalia. I recognized several of the house fragrances. *Vert. Blanc. Rouge. Noir.* All, I knew, created between 1919 and 1922, still considered among the top ten scents of the industry, alongside such classics as Chanel No. 5, Shalimar, and Mitsouko. A woman sat perched behind a glass table. She wore a black shift, high heels, and a black scarf.

"I have an appointment with Jac L'Etoile. I'm Cassiopeia Vitt."

She rose from the table and, pushing on one of the mirrored panels, opened a doorway. I followed her into a long hallway that ended at a carved wooden door which she opened.

Jac L'Etoile waited to greet me.

She was lovely, with almond-shaped, pale green eyes, and an oval face framed by wavy mahogany-colored hair. Perhaps a bit older than me, maybe mid-forties, she sported a stylish white smock over black slacks and suede ballet slippers. She seemed entirely comfortable with herself and I kept telling myself that this woman was a direct descendent of a long line of perfumers stretching back to the late 1700s.

"*Bonjour*," the perfumer said, as she extended her hand. "Would you like some coffee or tea?"

I asked for coffee and the receptionist left for the refreshments.

"Welcome to my shop," Jac said, waving her arms.

Cabinets filled with hundreds of bottles of sparkling liquids in shades of yellow, amber, green, and brown lined one wall. A set of French doors opened into a lush courtyard filled with blooming flowers and verdant trees.

"Nicodème called and said to treat you like family."

"He's a dear old friend."

"Who seems to have a problem."

I nodded. "That he does."

"He also mentioned your love of perfume. Would you like a quick tour?"

I nodded. Absolutely.

"This," she said walking over to a wooden apparatus that filled a quarter of the room, "is the heart of what I do. The perfumer's organ."

Which I knew about. About eight feet long and six feet tall, made of poplar. Three-tierd, and instead of keys to play music, rows of glass vials lined up like soldiers, each of a different essence. Best guess? It looked like there were more than three hundred vials.

"We don't know who the cabinetmaker was," Jac said. "But according to my grandfather, it's as old as the shop. For centuries, perfumers have been practicing their craft in laboratories, like this one. Even though modern labs have stopped using perfume organs, for me there's no better way. As my brother used to say, 'perfume is about the past, about memories, dreams.'"

I couldn't disagree with that, and I admired her obvious love of her craft.

Jac spread her arms. "Every generation of perfumers in my family has used these same bottles." There was something both proud and forlorn about her statement. She caressed the organ's wood. "My brother created perfumes here. My father before him and his father before him, going all the way back to the first L'Etoile, who opened this store in 1770. Like all the early perfumers, he'd been a glove maker who used scent in order to imbue the kidskins with a more pleasant aroma. When he saw how well it pleased his clients, he added other scented products.   Candles, pomades, soaps, sachets, powders, skin oils, creams."

The door opened and the receptionist returned with a tray of china cups, a silver coffee pot, creamer, sugar bowl, and spoons.

"Shall we?" Jac asked and we returned to her desk.

Sitting opposite her, I declined sugar and milk and accepted the cup she offered and sipped the black coffee. Not surprisingly, it was not only delicious but exceptionally fragrant.

"What is in this to give it a scent?" I asked.

"Just a couple of cocoa beans. Do you like it?"

"Quite a lot."

"It's one of the first lessons a perfumer learns. How sometimes the smallest addition makes all the difference."

"That's true in life too."

She smiled. "And in business. I suppose you want to know about the Sabbat Box, and what I discovered from the samples."

I nodded.

"That was quite an investigation," she said. "I did the work about a year ago. Amazingly, it appeared one of the oils Nicodème sent me had many similarities with a fragrance I worked with six years ago. It's the same formula, with only a few variations. I still believe that can't be a coincidence. How familiar are you with chemical analyses and botanical properties?"

I shook my head. "Not much at all, beyond a fascination with the whole concept of perfume."

"When Nicodème sent me the samples I ran them through gas chromatography and mass spectrometry. In most cases it's used for drug detection, environmental analysis, and explosives investigations. But fragrance companies often employ them to study the competition's scents. In a matter of hours those machines can break down a rival's formula that took months to create."

"What did you learn?"

"We were able to identify several ingredients. A few from over a decade ago, then two more from a recent scientific breakthrough. Quite a surprise, actually, to find one particular substance there. Three years ago a botanist in Israel managed to grow two ancient plants that have been extinct for years. Because of that, their chemical fingerprints are now in a database." Jac found three sheets of paper. "Here is the analysis."

She handed them to me.

I glanced down at the information. Ten separate copy blocks, a large number of the words in Latin of whose meaning I had no idea. "I'm afraid I don't know what most of these are."

She held out her hand and I returned the sheets. "Both of those ancient, formerly-extinct plants were in the Sabbat Box. Some of the ingredients are harmless, or simple hallucinogenics. But there are a few that can cause some potent reactions. Combinations and dosage is the key. With many of the vials, a small amount would cause adverse reactions—slight problems like headaches. A little more leads to severe neurological disorders. A little more and it can be fatal. The combinations of the plants and extracts in the box were surely once used for things like medicines, aphrodisiacs, even poisons. It's like a mobile pharmacy."

"Do some of them include the side effect of wild hallucinations?" I asked.

"Quite a few, in fact. Ancient priests were adept at mixing formulas to enable the user to enter into deep meditative states, supposedly so they could commune with the spirit world or dream prophecies. I've personally had contact with a formula like that. It caused what could have been mere hallucinations or," she glanced at me, "I'm not sure what your belief system is so you might be skeptical of this. Past life memories. All brought on by inhaling an ancient fragrance."

A day ago I would have dismissed what she just said as nonsense. But now I had a more open mind. "I don't *not* believe."

"Nicodème told me you'd had some unusual visions. Was it your first time?"

I nodded. "Initially I thought I'd had a simple hallucination. I'd been knocked unconscious during a robbery. But then I came in contact with some of the oil from one of the bottles and experienced a second and third incident."

"As someone who's been studying past life memories for the last six years, I'd be happy to help any way I can. There's an expert in New York City, Dr. Malachi Samuels, whom I've consulted several times. If there's something I can't help with, I can put you in touch with him."

I thanked her and we then focused on what I'd come to find out.

"The bottles in the box contained pure extracts of plants still used today in medicines," Jac said. "Belladonna, Datura, and mandrake are good for heart, lung, and nervous system issues, including heart failure resuscitation. In some cases they can even be utilized as antidotes to poisons. Because of a compound called tropane, which they contain, none of them should be taken internally. Even one dosage can cause permanent heart damage or death. Some people even drink wine infused with mandrake or henbane, but the dangers far outweigh the benefits.

"*Atropa belladonna* has a long history with the occult. *Atropos* was one of the three Fates whose name means *inevitable,* as she was the one who cut the thread of life causing death for humans. The drug was, and still is, used by shamans to open doorways between worlds. Nightshade, which was also in the Sabbat Box, is a vine with bright purple flowers and red berries. Every aspect of the plant is toxic. Medically it's used to heal bruises, swelling, sprains, and sores, but should never be burned as an incense or ingested."

Like I would. My work with the box was confined to a brief interaction, but even that was beginning to make me a little uneasy. I kept listening as she explained about *Datura stramonium,* the Devil's Trumpet, which was dangerous even to touch. It possessed many healing properties, but it also caused severe, unpredictable hallucinations that could last hours or days.

"Sometimes the taker had to be tied up to prevent him or her from hurting themselves or others," Jac said. "It was used by shamans and spiritualists to travel out of their bodies to the spirit world, for soul retrieval or to reverse curses set by ancestors. It's some potent stuff."

"It was in the box?"

She nodded. "And then there was henbane, which ancient Greeks used as a sedative. It was also popular as an aphrodisiac, added to love potions, beers, wines, and massage oils. It's toxic, hallucinogenic, and highly dangerous."

Which filled the glass vial resting in my pocket.

I removed the bottle, set it on the desk, and explained about the visions. Jac listened, then retrieved one of the plastic pipettes and drew a sample from the bottle, quickly opening, then replacing the cork stopper as we both held our breaths.

"It takes more than a quick whiff," I said. "But no point taking chances."

She deposited the sample into a vial and sealed the top.

"I'll take a look and see what's here. It could be a mixture. Of the samples I tested, seven bottles contain pure ingredients. Three held compounds with multiple elements, including some from the other bottles. One formula caused a deep meditative hallucinogenic state. A second was a powerful aphrodisiac. The third induced a semiconscious meditative state, possibly some sort of truth serum like ethanol, scopolamine, or amobarbital. The contents of that box are, without question, dangerous. If abused, the ingredients could be fatal." She pointed at the glass bottle. "I'd be careful with that stuff."

I re-pocketed the bottle, my mind processing all of the information. At present, the whereabouts of the Sabbat Box were unknown. It had been stolen, then re-stolen, and whoever stole it the second time was no friend of Nicodème or Antoine. Best guess? The thief had a use for the contents that didn't include murder, since there were surely easier ways to kill someone.

"I'll run some more tests and let you know what I find," Jac said. "In the meantime, I'm not a detective, but I have a friend who once was. He's helped me in the past. Nicodème suggested you might need some local knowledge."

She reached for a pad of paper, wrote down a name and phone number, then handed it to me.

Pierre Marcher.

I tucked the information into my pocket.

"You have quite a puzzle on your hands," Jac said.

That was an understatement.

Chapter 9

I LEFT THE PERFUME SHOP AND CHECKED MY PHONE TO SEE IF ANTOINE might have texted. He'd not, so I sent another message that I was available, then walked toward the Seine. Any other time the beauty of the river and the serenity of the surroundings would have soothed me, but not today. My phone vibrated and I checked the display, hoping to see a message from Antoine.

But it was Cotton.

Have you learned anything yet about your hallucinations?

On the train ride north I'd called and told him about the dreams, sharing my plans for Paris. He wasn't thrilled with the decision to purposely inhale from the bottle, but he trusted my judgement. As I did his. Another of the reasons we made a great team.

I replied that I'd seen Jac and typed out an abbreviated version of what the Sabbat Box contained then asked what he thought someone might do with such an assortment.

I'll have to think on that one. Keep in touch.

He wasn't much help, but he was also a long ways away and out of the loop. That was the thing about men. They were fixers. They liked to make bad situations better. Probably harkened back to the Stone Age and hunter gatherers and all that crap. But I rarely required a fixer. I preferred to solve my own problems. Which was another reason I loved Cotton. He was more a listener. That I could use and Cotton was really good at, as he put it, "keeping his mouth shut and his ears open."

I hesitated putting the phone away, allowing my fingers to linger on its surface. Though only symbolic, it was still a connection to him. Even though we were used to being apart, I missed him. It had been over two weeks since we'd seen each other last, and it would be at least that much or more before our next visit. I many times wondered what it would be like to be with him all the time. I'd never had that level of closeness with anyone. But, I'd already decided that he was the one man where that might be possible.

One day.

I crossed the Pont Carrousel. Though only late morning there were couples already out on the arched bridge, lingering, holding hands, some kissing. The city of lovers, right? Cliché, but true. I'd always felt comfortable here. I thought again about Cotton, still missing him, and the strange dreams. I still didn't want to call them memories.

So what were they?

I continued on into the Tuileries Garden and came out on the Rue Rivoli. I walked from there to Place Vendôme, home to the famed Ritz hotel and some of the most exclusive jewelry shops in the world. I'd been known to spend a little money there. Turning on Rue Danielle Casanova, I walked halfway down the block and found the entrance to the Du Lac Auction House.

My meeting with Claude Mantte was disappointing. I gleaned little that I didn't already know and I left in a black mood. For the third time I texted Antoine, who still hadn't responded. But this time I got an answer.

By way of a call.

"It's time we meet," he said.

"Are you all right? I left you on the ground to get help. But when I got back you were gone."

"Nicodème told me where you were headed. Go back to the perfume shop and wait outside. I'll be along shortly."

His tone bristled, but I ignored it and agreed to be there. It took me less than fifteen minutes to retrace my route. I stood outside the shop, across the street, watching for him. Finally, a black Citroën eased to the curb and the passenger-side door opened. Antoine was behind the wheel, with a bandage on the right side of his forehead, and another around his left wrist.

"Hop in."

I did and he drove off.

"I'm here," he said, without preamble, "because my brother,

Denton, is in Paris. I think he was behind the attack on us both."

"Are you okay?"

He gestured to his hand. "Banged up for sure. A hiker came along and helped me. They took me to the hospital in Monaco."

I had checked only in Nice.

"And you're all right?" he asked.

"I had some hallucinations after, and a headache."

"You mean like dreams, but more, as if you were actually there, living it out?"

I nodded slowly. "You too?"

"I've experienced it before. As I told you, the Sabbat Box belonged to my father. He kept it in our home for many years. Once, curiosity got the best of me, and I explored its contents. I sniffed from one of the bottles and passed out. I woke up with a memory of another time. I had been on a battlefield during World War I. In the trenches. A horrible place. There was shooting, death, then poisoned gas. It was so real. Almost overpowering."

"My dreams were more benign. I was a woman named Morgan le Fay. I was in a forest, with rain. There was a fortress that belonged to me, given to me by my half-brother, but he'd decided to take it back." I was a little embarrassed to continue, but knew I had to. "And I was making love to a man, there to protect me."

There had to be some logical explanation but, for the life of me, I couldn't think of one.

"Is that why you wanted the box back," I asked. "To experience more dreams."

He nodded. "And to find some answers. It's bothered me for a long time."

He navigated the traffic and I explained everything I'd learned about the box's ingredients, then I asked, "Why do you think your brother was behind the ambush and robbery?"

"Denton knows about the box and what the mixtures can do. He smelled them once too. He also knew who bought the box and that I was going to get it back. We spoke a few days ago."

"Why not just help you? Why attack you?"

"Because he knew that I wasn't going to hand it over to him. I don't trust him."

I was amazed. "But to attack you? Is he capable of that?" I had no siblings, but the idea of one doing anything so violent seemed inconceivable. "How did you know it was him?"

"He left a calling card."

He held out his wrist and showed me a blue string wristlet supporting a small metal charm.

"It's an evil eye," he said. "Our grandmother gave us each one."

He reached into his pants pocket and brought out an identical wristlet, the string circle severed. "It was lying on top of me when I woke up. His way of telling me to back off."

"Why does that box matter so much to him? Do you think he's planning on using those ancient oils?"

"I truly don't know."

He was quiet for the moment. I recalled what Cotton had told me about Denton Lussac. "Does your brother work for Lydia St. Benedict?"

"He does. And that's what's worrying me. I'm wondering if all this has something to do with the election."

Which I knew was only five days away. The campaign between President Casimir and his challenger, Lydia St. Benedict, had been one of the worst in French history. Charges and counter-charges had been flung by both sides. The polls were deadlocked, the country split 50/50 in a dead heat.

"The final debate is tomorrow night," he said.

"What could the Sabbat Box have to do with that?"

"My brother was once a wonderful person. But something happened to him, five years ago, after our father died. He was excluded from the will, banned from inheriting, and he took that hard. He resented me and our older brother and blamed us for Father's rebuke. He became unscrupulous, power hungry, and a liar, all of which makes him unpredictable and dangerous. He didn't follow me to Eze and take that box merely out of a sibling rivalry. Something is happening here and we have to find out what."

"We?"

"I need your help. This is way beyond me. Nicodème says you're a woman of skill and means. And that's exactly what I need."

Chapter 10

WE DROVE TO AN APARTMENT IN THE 16TH ARRONDISSEMENT THAT Antoine told me belonged to a friend who'd offered it for a few days. It sat on the second floor of a 19th century classic Belle Epoch dwelling, with high ceilings and tall windows that overlooked a courtyard planted with trees and a knot garden. Antoine's friend apparently loved books, the walls lined with shelves overflowing with volumes, new and old. Their presence made me miss Cotton even more, who loved nothing more than searching through antique shops and flea markets for rare first editions. Modern furniture offset the traditional moldings, parquet floors, and rugs. It was past lunch time and neither of us had eaten, so from groceries he had in the car we made cheese omelets. Antoine opened a bottle of Sancerre appropriated from the kitchen wine rack. Once the food was ready, we took our plates and glasses and sat down at the dining room table.

"We're going to have to confront Denton," he said. "But he's not going to just open up and admit to what he did. That's not his nature. Thankfully, he's something of a braggart."

"Unlike you?"

"We're different in so many ways. But he might hint at his plans with the right prompting."

"To you?"

Antoine shook his head. "Not a chance. To him, I'm the enemy."

"How well do you know the people in his life? Are there women?"

"He's gay."

"Are there men?"

"I'm sure there are quite a few."

"Anyone that he's close to?"

Antoine frowned. "I have no idea. We've been estranged for a long time."

"Yet you spoke last week."

"I had to know if he'd gone after the box."

"Apparently not."

He nodded. "Not until yesterday, at least."

I agreed. Denton Lussac had to be found. And fast. I'd heard Cotton lament many times about involving locals in an operation. Rarely did they prove helpful. But this was not a United States Justice Department mission. And I wasn't an intelligence agent. Help here would be appreciated. I remembered the card in my pocket Jac L'Etoile had given me with Pierre Marcher's name and number. I found it and made the call on Nicodème's cell phone. Marcher answered on the second ring. I explained who I was and who'd recommended him.

"Anything for Jac," he said. "And she called and said I might hear from you."

He agreed to meet us within the hour at a local bistro.

The Café Winka.

Antoine and I entered the café and I searched the faces. The tables were nearly full but there was no question which one accommodated Pierre Marcher. He stood as we approached. He was short and slim with slicked-back black hair. He wore stylish wire-rimmed glasses and where his right eyebrow should have been there was a ragged white scar, like a crack in an otherwise fine piece of glazed pottery. His navy suit fit him well and his starched white shirt looked fresh.

"Inspector Marcher?" I asked.

"Marcher is fine. I'm not with the police anymore."

We took a seat at the table. A waiter appeared and both Antoine and I ordered coffee. It took the better part of a half hour for us to explain the situation and what we knew, as well as an outline of what we needed to find out.

"I know of your brother," Marcher told Antoine.

I knew what he meant. *Officially.* As a former cop.

Antoine seemed to get it too. "My brother's reputation is not good, so feel free to say whatever is on your mind. We haven't gotten along for years, nor has he with anyone else in the family. There's little you could say that would shock or disappoint me."

"He was on our radar. We questioned him a few times, but could never amass enough evidence to charge him."

Antoine nodded. "You mean the extortion."

I looked at him. "What are you talking about?"

"There were rumors that my brother blackmailed several members of the National Assembly."

"He did just that," Marcher said. "Unfortunately, we were never able to learn the entire story. None of the members of Parliament cared to press charges. For good reason, I assume, since the dirt was true."

"My brother is for hire to the highest bidder. And this political season, Madame St. Benedict seems to be the one with the deepest pockets. He's been working with her for some time. The media has wondered how she's managed to counter Casimir's dirty tricks? Her gains in the polls are all thanks to Denton."

The election had been all the news for the past few weeks. Despite being in office for almost five years, President Yves Casimir had never connected with the people. Terrorism had crippled the French tourist trade, the economy lagged, immigration remained a continuing problem. Relations with the EU and America were strained. Instead of calming fears or providing hope, Casimir chose an indifferent approach, one that had made him immensely unpopular. His opponent, Lydia St. Benedict, seemed his antithesis. A widow, whose husband had died in a terrorist attack in Nice. She'd been at a hotel with their two children, who were in bed with colds, when her husband had gone out for a walk and never returned. What worked against her was inexperience. Along with the fact that Casimir had a reputation for playing hard ball. The pundits were waiting to see if Madame St. Benedict could beat Casimir at his own game. The election loomed less than a week away, the candidates' last national debate tomorrow night.

"Do you think your brother is after Casimir?" I asked.

Antoine shrugged. "There's no telling what he's after, but that Sabbat Box has something to do with it. He came after me for a reason. It's the only thing that makes sense."

"Can you help us out?" I said to Marcher.

The inspector never hesitated. "I thought you'd never ask."

I understood. "Unfinished business?"

"Something like that."

I recalled everything that Jac L'Etoile had told me about the powerful hallucinations inside the box. It was clear that Marcher was thinking too. I could almost read his mind. Finally, he glanced my way.

"A man like Yves Casimir is vulnerable in many different ways. Which means a man like Denton Lussac has a fertile field to plow. I agree with Antoine. This is much bigger than finding an old box."

Chapter 11

WE DECIDED TO SPLIT UP.

Too many possibilities for where Denton might be existed for all of us to stay together. Marcher was going to stake out Denton's residence and follow him or whoever he could find there. Antoine and I headed to Lydia St. Benedict's home. Marcher had learned through his police connections that the candidate was there, preparing for the upcoming final debate, her children with their grandmother during the final stretch of the race.

St. Benedict lived thirty minutes outside of Paris in Barbizon, a small town on the edge of the Fontainebleau forest, once a favorite hunting ground for the kings of France. The trip took an hour in Antoine's car. Traffic had been bad until we came clear of the suburbs. I'd visited the palace of Fontainebleau several times. For someone like me, with an interest in medieval architecture, the site was a must-see. Its famed château had served as a sovereign residence for over eight hundred years. The Capétiens, Valois, Bourbons, Bonapartes and Orléans all left their mark. Catherine de' Medici had made smart use of its secret passageways to spy on her husband and his mistress. Before being exiled to Elba, Napoleon abdicated there.

While finishing my PhD I'd spent several weeks at the Château de Fontainebleau and had come to know not only the buildings, but its forests, environs, and the town. The inn I frequented sat within walking distance to Lydia St. Benedict's home. I booked two rooms for the night and learned from the desk clerk that St. Benedict was at home. I showered, dressed, and we both ate a light supper of soup and salad at a nearby café. While eating I overheard the people at the next table, who seemed to be from St. Benedict's campaign retinue. They were upbeat, discussing their candidate's poll numbers, all of them feeling good about the debate tomorrow night. We left the café around a quarter to nine.

The walk to St. Benedict's house took ten minutes.

It sat among the trees, off the road. Lights burned both downstairs and upstairs. Otherwise the house seemed quiet. One car sat parked in the driveway.

"Should we ring the bell?" Antoine asked.

"I've always liked the direct approach. But let me do this. We don't know who else is there."

He seemed to understand. "Denton?"

I nodded. "Better you wait out here. As you said, you're not the right person to approach him."

He nodded.

I left him in the trees, walked to the front door, and rang the bell. No answer. I waited, but no one came. No butler or maid? Surely St. Benedict employed people. I stepped away from the door and signaled for Antoine to stay put. I then walked around to the side and explored the grounds. The house was typical of the mid-1700s, probably once owned by someone of importance close to the royal family. The walls were a warm, creamy gray stone which I knew was from the Oise quarries about twenty-five miles outside of Paris.

I rounded the far side and saw an open window on the ground floor. I approached and peeked in at the kitchen. The ancient stone hearth was still intact with a cast iron pot hanging from a hook. Judging from the elaborate stainless steel stove, the hearth was no longer utilized. But clearly a lot of the old charm had survived renovations.

Still no one around.

I decided to be bold and climbed inside.

I crept through the kitchen and explored the rest of the rooms downstairs. A fire burned in the living room hearth—unusual if no one was home. A half full stem of red wine rested on a coffee table. Beside that was a tumbler holding a quarter inch of brown liquor. A sniff told me it was Scotch.

Indentations on the Regency couch seemed to indicate that two people had been seated there not long before. The dining room loomed empty but the chairs were haphazardly pulled out. Papers were strewn across the top and a laptop was open displaying a frozen image of St. Benedict at a lectern. An indicator showed the video at half over. Everything here seemed like unfinished business.

I walked down a short corridor to an empty library, then up the stairs. Each of the four bedrooms were empty. Two were children's rooms. A third, a guest room, seemed in use by a man judging from the clothes and shoes. The last bedroom, at the opposite end of the hall, was the master, which smelled of perfume. Up one more flight of stairs and I found a warren of servants' rooms and a playroom for children.

No one there either.

Back downstairs, I stood in the foyer and absorbed the atmosphere. If there was life in this house I couldn't hear or see it. I walked through the rooms once more and a thought occurred to me. Old houses like this usually came with a basement and perhaps even a sub-basement. From what I knew of 17th century architecture, most entrances to the sub-levels were off the kitchen. I returned there and found a staircase leading down to a lit, ventilated, truncated basement. There were storage rooms, a wine cellar, even a laundry. Its size was smaller than expected. Typically, a basement stretched across the house's entire footprint, part of its stone foundation.

But not here.

Dead silence enveloped me.

Then I began to hear sounds.

Muffled.

Hard to identify.

I shut my eyes and listened.

They came again.

More distinct.

I crept close to the perimeter of the exterior walls, nestling my ear to the stone.

Nothing.

Had I imagined it?

I returned upstairs and re-walked the first floor, figuring dimensions, counting footsteps, eye-balling measurements and comparing them to the basement where I'd just been. I ascertained that the space I'd just explored in the basement was under the kitchen, the living room, and the dining room but had not extended under the sun room or the library or the bathroom off of it.

Interesting.

Sometimes a degree in medieval architecture came in handy. I knew that châteaus built before 1900 often came with hidden chambers. Sometimes they'd served as private spaces. Entrances to those secret rooms were often hidden behind false walls, many times inside closets or behind shelving or cabinetry. All of the tropes in books, movies, and novels were true. For the sake of thoroughness I investigated the shelves in the library, but none of them sprang open. I stepped back into the living room and looked around one last time.

Something felt wrong about this whole place.

And even though I didn't know Lydia St. Benedict, I felt compelled to make sure all was well with her.

My gaze focused on the hearth where the fire had become just burning embers. The fireplace itself was twice normal size—large enough for someone to step into provided they stooped over. I walked back to the library which had the same tall ceilings and oversized fireplace. Remnants of the last fire that had burnt there were cold to the touch, though the scent of smoke and burnt wood lingered. I stepped around the andirons, into the hearth, and ducked inside. The walls were typically scorched. Ashes littered the grate.

Then I saw them.

Footprints in the ash.

One set of a woman's, the other a man's.

I pushed on the right wall. Nothing happened. Nor did the wall at the back of the enclosure give. But the left wall moved. It opened without a sound, easily swinging inward and revealing a stone staircase. A breeze of cool air wafted up without even a hint of a musty odor. No cobwebs anywhere. This was an active passageway. I made my way down the stone staircase to an oak door, complete with an iron ring and hinges, devoid of rust.

I grabbed the ring and gently pushed.

It moved inward without a sound.

Enough for me to see something astonishing.

Chapter 12

A DUNGEON.

Or more accurate, a sexual dungeon.

A playroom, if I remembered the correct term.

The lights were dim, the shadows heavy. Fully equipped too. Shackles on the wall. Iron cage. Racks of whips. Chains. Ropes. Benches. And Lydia St. Benedict, spread-eagle atop a black X, her waist, wrists, and ankles restrained on a St. Andrew's Cross. Not that I had ever partaken, but I wasn't ignorant to such things either. Named for the *crux decussata*, the diagonal cross upon which St. Andrew died, adapted by the erotic world as a device of pain and pleasure.

St. Benedict was naked, except for a black leather collar. A man stood before her, holding a leather riding crop. And not just any man. The same height, build, and face as Antoine, only a little younger.

His brother, Denton.

Who used the crop to tease her breasts. My first instinct was to rush in and stop the violation. But I realized that I was the intruder here. This was a private place and St. Benedict did not appear to be in jeopardy. Quite the contrary. She seemed to enjoy his titillations. What caused me concern was the tripod that stood off to one side that held a silver cellphone, its camera aimed at the scene.

Troubling.

But again, who was I to judge?

On a table I saw the Sabbat Box, a few of its bottles out, but still corked. That raised the most serious warning signs, considering their powerful effects. The doorway where I stood lay in the shadows, about ten meters away from the unfolding sexual antics. Neither of them noticed me. I continued to stare, both embarrassed by my momentary voyeurism and enthralled by the scene. I knew people who enjoyed this sort of thing. That enticing mixture of pain and pleasure, dominance and submission, give and take.

Lydia St. Benedict's eyes stayed unfocused and downcast. Denton seemed a portrait of control. Emotionless and powerful. He stopped his taunting and turned. We saw each other at the same time. My first instinct was to drop back and pull the door closed, but I did not move.

"Come closer," he said.

I stepped into the dungeon.

"This is not what it seems."

He stepped toward me and had not asked my name, nor even seemed surprised that I was here. But why would he? If Antoine was right, this was the man who attacked us on the Philosopher's Walk. So he would know my face.

He came close and stopped.

"I'm Denton Lussac."

Perhaps diplomacy was the call of the day.

"Cassiopeia Vitt."

His right hand whipped upward in a flash.

The metal end of the whip caught me on the right temple.

And the world dissolved to black.

So much for diplomacy.

My head ached.

Slowly, I opened my eyes. I tried to raise an arm to examine my scalp but couldn't move either of my hands. Ties around my wrists held them back. My feet were likewise restrained. Then I realized something filled my mouth.

Denton stared at me. "Have you ever experienced a ball gag before?"

I slowly shook my head.

"Its purpose is most often humiliation. Your mouth is partially forced open and the rubber ball prevents you from effectively swallowing. Spit builds up beneath your tongue and eventually drools out the sides of your mouth. Since your hands are restrained, there's nothing free to wipe your face with. Incredibly, this simple violation of hygiene can break a person down."

His words came matter-of-factly, without a single measure of concern. Thankfully, I'd been in worse situations and, more than that, I refused to let this prick get to me.

"Pain is an offshoot of humiliation," he said. "Depending on the size of the ball, the size of your mouth, and how hard the ties are fastened, the ball can force your jaw to open unnaturally wide. Which doesn't sound like a big deal, but, with time, it can become excruciating. And not all that much time needs to pass either. Adding to the humiliation is that you don't speak clearly when the ball is removed. It's quite the toy."

He slipped the ball from my mouth.

I swallowed hard. Though I was at his mercy, bound to one of the iron chairs, I wasn't helpless. Instead, I was taking in everything around me. Preparing. Planning. Waiting.

Across the room Lydia St. Benedict lay naked in a cage, asleep it appeared. Such a strange sight to see a candidate for the presidency of France in such a helpless condition. Her image was one of a type-A personality. An alpha female. In total control. But then I realized it all made sense. Her apparent sexual tastes relied on trust, safety, and surrender, overlapped by an element of *being* in charge. Dominant and submissive. Unequal roles that led to arousal and satisfaction. A risk-aware consensual game, with the submissive being in name only, as the ultimate control rested with the one receiving the pain and pleasure. Not the other way around. Too bad most French voters wouldn't grasp the truth of the situation. If they saw her now, it would most likely be political suicide.

And that thought made me angry on her behalf.

Denton stepped close to St. Benedict and whispered through the cage bars, "Lydia?"

She opened her eyes and looked around, seemingly confused. "I don't feel well. What's wrong with me? Denton? Please, tell me."

He opened the cage.

"Why is my head all fuzzy?"

She sounded like a small child. Then I realized she was drugged. No question. Probably something from the Sabbat Box. I wondered which of the concoctions he'd used. And I recalled Jac's warning that mixing the ingredients could be both dangerous and fatal. I stared across at the tripod and noticed that the silver cell phone was gone. The Sabbat Box remained on the table, a few more of its stoppered bottles out.

St. Benedict staggered as if in a trance. Her head drooped to one side. Denton's caretaker mask was gone, replaced by cold, calculating eyes and a stiff frame. I pulled on my restraints, itching to place him in the cage she'd just vacated. He'd clearly violated the enormous trust she'd given him.

"What are you doing?" I asked.

He glanced back at me. "Winning the election."

He helped St. Benedict out of the dungeon and wrapped a blanket around her nakedness. She never turned around, never saw me, and had no idea I was even there.

My mind raced.

Denton Lussac was not working *for* St. Benedict. He was working for her opponent, President Yves Casimir. What better way to tip a close election than through a deep personal slander. Lydia St. Benedict's sexual proclivities would be, at a minimum, horribly embarrassing. True, the French were liberal in their sexual attitudes. A lot was forgiven. Having an affair or a love child hardly raised an eyebrow. But would the electorate accept that the woman running to be one of the most powerful leaders in the EU was a submissive who allowed—even enjoyed—her partner to physically and mentally dominate her? Not the image any national leader wanted. And in a close election it could provide a few percentage points of swing, making all the difference.

The oak door closed.

Then it reopened.

Denton stepped across and re-inserted the ball gag into my mouth. "I almost forgot."

He left.

Silence reigned.

I was trapped.

Chapter 13

A HALF HOUR PASSED BEFORE DENTON RETURNED.

Alone.

My head still ached. Drool oozed from the sides of my mouth and had for the past few minutes. I studied him. He and Antoine were similar in the face, the same dark hair, powerful features and piercing brown eyes. But from the bumps on his nose and a scar above his eyebrow, I guessed he'd been in his share of fights. Unlike Antoine, this man's countenance exuded more of a sense of entitlement. I'd seen the look before. That I'm-smarter-than-you-are-and-always-will-be arrogance.

"There's no one here, but the three of us. No houses nearby. Stone walls and earth all around you. I'm going to ungag you. But let's not wake Lydia with any screaming."

Like I would. Asshole. I don't scream.

He released the ball gag from around my head, grabbed a towel from a rack and wiped my face of the spittle. I swallowed. I never realized how satisfying that simple act could be. My jaw was sore and I worked out the kinks.

He motioned to the room. "You invaded our private sanctuary."

"And you stole that box over there with the potions from your brother and kicked me in the head. Then you drugged St. Benedict with them. So how about we cut the crap."

His smile disgusted me. "Touché, Ms. Vitt."

He motioned to the box. "My dear brother thought it his duty to retrieve it. Some sort of family heirloom. Like always, though, Antoine never could grasp the bigger picture."

"And that would be political extortion?"

I was baiting him.

He stepped over to the table and lifted one of the bottles. "These are powerful potions. Much more powerful than anything we have today. The ancients knew their chemistry." He laid the bottle down. "Tell me why you're here."

My head remained foggy from the pop to my temple, but I was pretty sure I'd correctly assembled the pieces of this deceptive game.

"Is this her thing?" I asked.

He shrugged. "We all have our secrets. The madam likes her play in a particular variety. I merely oblige her."

"Apparently she trusts you."

He chuckled. "Obviously. That's the whole idea. She submits, I dominate. She trusts, I take advantage. The amazing part is that I helped bring her to within a statistical tie with the current president of France. A masterful campaign, if I do say so. She might even win—"

"If you weren't working for the other side."

"Precisely."

"She'll never know until it's way too late, will she? Let me guess. The final debate is tomorrow night. The election less than a week away. So you'll leak that video, what, three days from now? The internet will explode. Her image of a strong, forceful leader, a family woman, the person to lead France after the disaster of Casimir will be gone. It won't change a lot of minds, but it could change enough to swing a few percentage points against her. That's all you need to win."

He pointed a finger at me. "Sit tight. Don't go anywhere." He smiled at his own joke. "I'm going to check on Lydia, then I'll be back to deal with you."

He left the dungeon.

What a mess. Hopefully, Antoine would head this way at some point. All I had to do was buy some time. But I was strapped at the wrists and ankles to an iron chair. I shut my eyes and tried to calm myself with images of Cotton. Our intimate experiences with each other couldn't be more different than what occurred in this place. But to each his or her own. Sex for the sake of sex? For the high, the escape, the release? Something to be said for that. But there was also sex used to prove power, to show strength, to satiate physical desire, to establish position, calm fears, debase, or define. Not all of which was good. Then there was sex simply for the connection, the celebration of emotion, a way to become closer, to explore and understand another's psyche, to delight in what two people can do to and for each other. That's what Cotton and I shared. Sure, we took chances, but we never pushed boundaries.

Unlike Denton Lussac.

Thoughts of Morgan le Fay appeared in my mind.

Flashes from the dream.

What was happening to me? Was I actually seeing the past? If so, those visions were beginning to affect my thinking. From what I knew about reincarnation, it's supposedly about repeating the past until you finished what was started. Fulfilling a karmic destiny. Righting wrongs. Redeeming yourself and learning lessons. What was the point of my past life? If it were mine at all.

The oak door reopened and Denton returned.

"Miss me?" he asked.

I did not answer.

"When I took the box back at Eze, I was in a bit of a rush. I failed to notice one of the bottles was gone. Antoine has the curiosity of a corpse, so I'm assuming you have it. Do you?"

I remained silent.

"Of course that was a rhetorical question. When I strapped you into that chair I noticed something in your pocket."

He fished the bottle from my pocket. "Let me guess. You're thinking, how do I get out of here? I need to get Madame Benedict to a hospital. Call the police. Save possibly the next president of France from herself, and the man she believes is orchestrating her political triumph, but who is actually creating her downfall. But, unfortunately, Madame Benedict will recall nothing of what just happened. A side effect of the drug-induced stupor she currently finds herself in. And the best part?"

I waited.

He displayed the bottle from my pocket.

"These concoctions are pure organic. Nature's own. They leave no chemical residue. No signature. Nothing to find in the blood or tissue. Madame Benedict will have no idea what came over her. But you." He pointed my way again. "You are a different story."

"I didn't realize I had such a reputation."

"I made a call while I was upstairs earlier. The *Direction Générale de la Sécurité Extérieure* is familiar with your reputation. You're a known commodity. I'm told you've been involved in several incidents that had global implications. And wealthy too. Your family's concerns are quite profitable. And, on top of all that, you're building a medieval castle.

That sounds impressive."

I matched his sarcasm with my own. "Would you like to contribute to the building fund?"

"Any other time, perhaps. But I have an election to lose."

"Was it President Casimir's idea for you to double cross St. Benedict?"

"Actually, it was mine. But he pays well."

His chattiness concerned me. Apparently, he did not intend for me to leave this dungeon alive. He examined all sides of the bottle he'd taken from me.

I saw something in his eye and had to ask, "You've experienced the effects, haven't you?"

He nodded. "Quite the trip. I was someone of great importance. A warrior. In a fight, then in a fortress, making love to a beautiful woman."

That sounded familiar.

"The woman have a name?"

He stared at me. "Morgan le Fay."

I fought my disgust. "Did you have a name?"

"Kaz of Gormet."

Fascinating. We were both in the same loop.

"Which bottle did you inhale?" I asked. He did not answer, so I tried, "How many trips did you take?"

"Two." He displayed the bottle again. "I'm assuming you've been doing some sniffing of your own. Which explains why you kept it."

Kaz of Gormet versus Helians of Gormet.

Antoine Lussac versus Denton Lussac.

Brother against brother.

In both times.

He lifted the towel he'd used to wipe my face and covered his mouth and nose. Then he uncorked the bottle and held it beneath my nostrils. "I'm afraid your time has come to an end."

I caught the distinctive waft.

"A little induces the visions," he said from behind the towel. "But a lot?"

His question hung in the air.

"A lot may kill."

I held my breath for as long as I could, then I had no choice.

I inhaled.

Chapter 14

*A*RTURIUS *HAS SENT A* GROUP OF *W*ARRIORS *TO TAKE MY CASTLE.* *They are camped beyond the walls, preparing for battle. Kaz of Gormet rides at their lead. Helians of Gormet stands in my workshop, dressed for battle. I dismiss my servant who has brought the news that the men beyond the walls seem to be readying an attack.*

"Do you think these plants will save you?" Helians asks me.

"Instead of you?"

He shrugs. "Lances and swords work far better than plants." He smiles. "But I must confess, I know nothing of the power of an herbalist's cabinet."

I love his open mind. So few men possess one. "Since ancient times there have been many among us schooled in the secrets of the flowers, herbs, mosses, and bark. Circe, Medea, Hecate—all the great queens—were practitioners. Great harm can be done to a great many, if one knows how."

"I've come to know that, if said by you, it's a true statement."

I smile at his confidence. "The Sorcerer, my teacher, showed me how to work with the gifts of the earth. There's one group, the Solanaceae plants, that are especially powerful. Included in them are belladonna, datura, henbane, mandrake, and nightshades."

I line up bottles on the table marked with those ingredients.

He watches, not in disdain or arrogance, but with fascination. "What can you do with these herbs and oils, my beautiful sorceress?"

"Defend my home."

"Against my brother and his armed men?"

"Hopefully. You do know this is not of my making. Your brother has never forgiven me. He is using this opportunity."

There are no secrets between us. Helians knows the history. Kaz, like his brother, carries the reputation of a brave, fearless man, but, unlike Helians, he's insensitive as a lover and thinks little of women, expecting all to bow and please him. Roughness and demands are his staples, and he sees me only as Arturius' half-sister, someone who might further his ambitions. Years ago, Kaz came to my home but, by the end of three days' time an animal sense warned me that he represented a threat. So I sent him away. He was not amused at being cast off and vowed revenge. Now he's found an ally in the anger of my half-brother and his wife.

"I didn't start this battle," I say to Helians again.

"Yet because of a slight that happened years ago, I could lose my brother."

"Who has treated you less than well. Who has—"

"Stop," Helians shouts. "He is still my brother."

"Your enemy," I say back.

"True, he's chosen Arturius over me," Helians says, sadness in his voice. "I wish this was different. A warrior owes his allegiance to the leader, over family, but if you had not cast Kaz out, Arturius would have surely chosen someone else to send. He assumes my brother has reason to fight harder than the rest. And he's correct."

I turn my attention to the bottles on the table and begin to mix the potion.

He watches me in silence.

"How will you use these concoctions?" he finally asks.

I point. "I'll soak rags with this one, then set them outside, by the gates. When Kaz's men approach, we'll set them on fire. All who breathe the smoke will fall asleep. Anyone who makes it through the gates will be met with a spray of another potion, doled out through bellows."

He seems intrigued. "What will those do?"

I look at him with grave eyes. "Render them helpless at first, then—" I pause. "They will forget."

He does not react. "Forget what?"

"The entire reason why they are here."

"I require something of you," he says. "I have never asked much from you, but on this day I ask that you not kill my brother."

"He threatens me. He wants to destroy me. And you ask me not to defend myself."

"On the contrary. I want you to defend yourself, as I will do on your behalf. But I do not want him killed. He is still my brother."

I nod.

"I want your solemn promise," he says.

I love this man, so I have no choice.

"And you have it."

Chapter 15

I OPENED MY EYES.

Someone was shaking me and saying my name.

"Helians?" I asked, still seeing the vision.

"Cassiopeia?"

I tried to clear the images from my brain, but it was harder this time to be free of the incredibly vivid hallucinations. I was shaken again. By a man. Helians?

The blur cleared.

Antoine was looking down at me. "Are you okay?"

I was free of the chair, lying on the dungeon floor. Sitting up, I shook out my arms and stretched. Antoine kept me steady.

"What happened?" he asked.

"Your brother tried to kill me." But thankfully he did not know enough about the bottles to realize that not all of them were deadly. "How long have I been out?"

"About a half hour. I had some trouble finding this place."

"How did you find it?"

"I was watching from one of the windows when Denton and St. Benedict emerged from the fireplace. I had to wait for them to leave before coming to find you. St. Benedict looked unsteady. Denton had to help her to a car." He looked around. "What is this place?"

My head cleared.

"A fun palace," I said, before telling him what happened, finishing with, "Lydia St. Benedict is in deep trouble."

The last bits of the dream stuck in my mind.

Brother against brother.

"We have to find St. Benedict."

An hour and a half later we were driving across Paris, through more traffic. I'd called Marcher during the drive and he'd learned that St. Benedict was at her Paris apartment in an upscale building located across the Seine from the Eiffel Tower. Denton had taken my bottle, so there was no way for me to experience any more dreams. Which was frustrating, as I felt like there was something unfinished in the past. Was the castle retaken? Had anything Morgan le Fay done worked? What happened with the brothers? It all seemed incomplete, but Antoine had meant well in trying to revive me.

Marcher was waiting for us when we found the address. Though the hour was late, television vans were parked down the street, the media camped out and held back by tape draped down the sidewalk. The building's main entrance was manned by uniformed security. Marcher stepped off to the side and started making phone calls trying to find someone to let us in. Somewhere inside was Lydia St. Benedict and Denton Lussac and the possibility existed that her entire candidacy was about to be compromised.

Marcher motioned for us to come toward him.

We hurried over.

"You're in," he said. "But hurry, before they change their mind. I'll stay here."

Antoine and I rushed across the street. The security men stopped us long enough to check IDs, then they let us pass, telling us to take the elevator to the eighth floor. There, another security guard directed us to an apartment door. Inside, Lydia St. Benedict waited.

Along with Denton.

The candidate looked quite different than in the dungeon. Now fully clothed, her hair and makeup perfect. Her face set with the countenance of a cheetah. She carried herself with a practiced air of confidence, the chin tilted slightly skyward, the lips pursed in a stern expression.

"May I help you?" St. Benedict said in French. "The police say that I should speak with you."

I watched as the two brothers appraised one another, neither saying a word.

"You must be Antoine," St. Benedict said. "Denton just told me you are his brother. A pleasure to meet you."

They shook hands.

"My name is Cassiopeia Vitt," I said. "Is that name familiar? Is my face familiar?"

"Neither is. Should they be?"

I ignored the question, which I could see irritated her.

"I must ask that you come to the point," St. Benedict said. "I have much to do, and I only agreed to this because of police insistence. They said the matter was important."

Her tone carried the snap of a whip.

Not a speck of recognition hovered in St. Benedict's eyes. Either she was really good, which was a definite possibility, or she had no memory of the past few hours. Denton, on the other hand, knew exactly what had transpired.

So much about him reminded me of Kaz from the hallucination. Though I'd not seen the man, Morgan's memories of him had flooded through my brain. His look, feel, voice, wants, desires. It was like I knew him, but I didn't. Both Kaz and Denton were on a quest for power at the expense of a woman. Like Morgan, St. Benedict was going to be branded a witch, only of a different kind, and her enemy was going to attempt to burn her at only a proverbial stake. But a stake nonetheless, her annihilation to be witnessed by an entire nation.

Unless I could stop it.

The Sabbat Box lay on the coffee table.

I turned to Denton. "Where's the video?"

"What video," St. Benedict asked.

"Yes, Miss Vitt," Denton added. "What video?"

I stared him down. "Is that how we're going to play this?"

"What are you talking about?" Denton asked, incredulity in his voice.

"Does President Casimir already have it," I asked.

"I think I should call in my security detail and have you both removed," St. Benedict said.

Denton found his phone. "I can make that call."

"I saw your dungeon," I said to St. Benedict.

Shock filled her face. "How?"

"I was in your house. I saw you there"—I pointed at Denton—"with him. You were tied to a St. Andrew's Cross. Naked."

I definitely now had her attention so I added, "He was filming you. On a phone."

"That's a lie," Denton said.

The man had not used his own phone, which he still held. Black. Wrong color.

"My apologies," I said, in a heartfelt voice. "I am so sorry, Madame. But he did film you."

My gaze drifted to the Sabbat Box, the bottles nestled tight in their individual compartments. The one I'd kept since Eze, the one Denton had taken, had been added back to the collection. I reached for it.

"Don't touch that," Denton said.

I ignored him.

"What's going on?" St. Benedict asked, her voice strained, almost frightened.

"He's not on your side," I said to her again.

She seemed to be listening to me. I took a chance and asked, "Have you seen visions?"

No reply.

"I've seen them," I offered. "Of the past. So real, as if I was there."

She nodded. "I have too."

"I need to go back there," I said.

"For what?"

"Answers."

"You can't allow this," Denton said, his mouth twisted into a sour line.

"I can do as I please," St. Benedict told him, her voice rising.

"You're going to listen to these people?"

"Yes, I am." She paused. "For the moment."

Denton did not challenge her.

"All right, Ms. Vitt," St. Benedict said. "You have one opportunity to explain yourself."

I reached down and removed the bottle. "You're going to have to trust me."

"I know nothing about you."

I removed the cork, inhaled, then replaced it, handing the bottle to her.

"Time for us both to learn."

Chapter 16

HELIANS LIES ON THE BED, BLEEDING FROM HIS WOUNDS.

They're severe. Life threatening.

Beyond my skills.

The battle is over and men are dead from both sides. Many more are injured. Kaz survived with barely a scratch. He's busy securing my fortress. I can only imagine what he's thinking. His plan to expose me as a witch and return my home to Arturius, hopefully garnering many favors in return.

I find a vial off the shelf, open it, then wet my fingers with its contents. I rub them over Helians' busted lips, then on the wounds that are still bleeding. Almost immediately the blood thickens and stops flowing. His face is deathly pale, but slowly color returns to his whitened cheeks.

My home remains under siege.

I have to stop Kaz.

I step back to my workshop and find my potion box. I remove three bottles, set them on the table, and mix the ingredients. One drop is strong. Five drops could easily cause a man to black out. More? Hard to say what will happen.

How will I get Kaz to take it?

I smile.

That is easy.

I find him with a few of his men. I bow to no man, but now I bow to him. "I fear your brother has passed on, Lord Kaz."

I bob my head in further deference.

"He never should have stood against me," he says.

I raise my head. "You speak the truth, my Lord. But I am a naïve woman, incapable of accomplishing much without the guidance of a man. With my apologies, I've brought a draught so we may drink to peace and the open surrender of my home to you."

He laughs. "You think me a fool, witch? I know of your potions. I'll be glad to accept a drink in peace and surrender, provided you drink first."

I motion and one of the servants brings a tray with wine and two goblets. Both are filled and I gesture that the choice is his. He smiles and selects one, which he hands to me. I take a long sip and swallow. "I'm not afraid of this ambrosia, my Lord. You have won your prize, I concede that. You are the victor this day."

I sip more wine and bow my head again.

Kaz lifts the second goblet. "To my brother. May his dishonor be wiped from his soul as he ascends to be judged by the Lord Almighty."

He brings the edge of the silver rim to his lips and drinks.

"Send your men away, my Lord. They are no longer required here. You not only have command of this fortress, but its lady as well." I toss him a smile. "I give myself to the victor."

He gets the message. "Are you offering yourself willingly?"

I nod. "I am in awe of your power and strength. I cannot help but do what is proper and give myself to you, as victor."

I watch, confident what this weak, vain soul will do.

And he does not disappoint me.

He dismisses his men, sending them back outside the walls. I gesture, then lead him to my bedchamber and refill his goblet. He begins to remove his breastplate. I offer him the wine, which he refuses.

"I'll take yours."

I smile. "As you wish, my Lord."

Though his mind screams caution, his eyes are full of lust. He wants me, and desire is the killer of reason. He takes my goblet and downs the contents in one swallow. I step to the bed, suggesting that he should finish undressing. He removes more of his armor. His face and chest are covered in sweat, his long hair matted with blood to his head.

"I have a bath ready for you," I tell him.

"That would be welcomed." He pauses. "Before I take you."

He continues to undress. I find myself admiring his strong, virile body. Similar to Helians and, if only physical appearance defined a man, Kaz would be a worthy specimen.

"Why don't you undress," he says.

"I will, my Lord. After your bath."

He smiles, standing there naked, proud of himself. I take his hand and lead him into the adjacent room where the warm water awaits. With no hesitation, he climbs into the tub and settles into the steaming liquid. Some of it spills over to the floor.

"Why don't you join me?" he says.

I walk around behind him and begin to massage his shoulders. The muscles are knotted, firm and tight, like hemp. He angles his head back, eyes closed. His breath deepens to long, full inhales. He is relaxing. Some of it voluntary, most thanks to the ingredients I'd added to the bath, knowing that they would seep through the skin and work their way straight to his head.

And they are.

His head droops to one side.

I make sure that it stays above the water, then I leave the room, hastening to Helians. He lies still where I left him. He will not last much longer. I sit on the edge of the bed and cradle his head in my lap.

"I've avenged you," I tell him.

"Did . . . you kill him?"

Tears form in my eyes. "No, my love. My promise was kept."

His hand caresses my arm. I hold him closer. I will truly miss this man.

"With soft gray eyes she gloomed . . . and glowered. With soft red lips . . . she sang a song. What man . . . might gaze upon her face . . . nor fare along."

I'm amazed. This man of fight and violence, citing poetry?

"I wrote it . . . for you, my love," he says. "A poem of . . . how . . . I feel."

"Is there more?"

"But when Morgan . . . with lifted hand, moved down the hall . . . they louted low. For she was Queen of Shadowland . . . that woman of snow."

He stares up at me.

"You are . . . a goddess. I'll wait for you . . . Morgan," he says with a ragged breath.

"Do you believe in the goddess?" I ask, surprised.

I know Helians had been brought up to believe in a wrathful,

Christian god, not in the idea that we pass from this life to another and another until we've accomplished all that it is our fate to achieve.

"I haven't been yours for these . . . past moons without . . . picking up some of your beliefs." He raises a hand and pushes my curls up behind my ear so he can look straight into my face. "You have given me . . . much joy, as I hope . . . I have you. As I hope . . . we will again."

I lean down and press my lips to his. A terrible darkness swallows me. My eyes feel the unaccustomed dampness of heavy grief. I keep him in my arms until he is no longer breathing, then I weep even more. The only man who means something to me is gone. I lay his head back on the bed and stand.

"Goodbye, my love."

I walk back to the bath, where Kaz still lies in the warm water. I cup some of it in my hands and splash it to his face. He rouses, blinks the moisture from his eyes, and focuses on me.

"Do I know you?" he says.

Chapter 17

I AWOKE.

A stale, poisonous taste had settled in my mouth. Surprisingly, little fear lingered from the experience, only a pause, a sense of relief and understanding, my mind a blur of questions.

Madame St. Benedict was bent over me, concern in her eyes. "Are you all right?"

My mind returned to the present, though thoughts from the past lingered. "How long have I been out?"

"Ten minutes."

Antoine stood a few feet away, Denton beside him.

I pushed myself up from the carpet.

"Where were you?" St. Benedict asked.

"Back a long time ago."

"You don't actually believe anything this woman says?" Denton asked. "She's clearly delusional from what she smelled."

"What's a long time ago?" St. Benedict asks, ignoring her aide.

"I'm not sure. There was a mention of a man named Arturius. And Morgan le Fay."

"She never existed," Denton spit out. "She's a fictional character."

"Who says?" I pointed out.

Denton shook his head. "You can't be serious. You're delusional from the effects of whatever is in that bottle. That's all."

But I saw Madame St. Benedict did not agree. So I asked her, "What did you see in your visions?"

"Things that were so real, so immediate, that they could not be dreams."

"And they happened when you and Denton were . . . interacting?"

She nodded. "I smelled from one of the bottles too."

"Madame St. Benedict," Denton said. "This is ludicrous. I implore you to call the security detail and have these people removed."

"Why are you here?" St. Benedict asked me.

Images of the dream were fading, but some of the memory lingered. "You're in danger."

"Enough of this." Denton darted toward the door.

Antoine cut him off with a tackle to the floor. The two brothers wrestled before Antoine planted a fist into his brother's face and Denton went still. St. Benedict did not move, allowing the fight.

"He's working for the other side," I told her. "He was filming you in the dungeon. I assume he's going to release the video sometime between now and the election next week."

St. Benedict seemed confused. "He's worked hard for me. Most of my success is attributed to him."

"What better way to gain your trust?" I said.

I could see that she agreed.

"Is that why you began a personal relationship," I asked.

She nodded. "I did trust him. Totally."

I heard the betrayal in her voice. A deep, visceral hurt that reached down to her core. She obviously believed what I was saying.

"Search him," I said.

Antoine rifled through his brother's pockets and found two cell phones.

One I recognized.

"It's the silver one," I said. "He used it in the dungeon."

Antoine swiped the screen. "It's password protected."

No surprise.

"We can only hope he's not turned anything over to the Casimir campaign yet," I said.

"I doubt he has," St. Benedict muttered. "We were scheduled to return to the country house later today for another . . . private session." She paused. "They relax me. I thought the experience would help before the debate. I imagine he would have filmed that too."

"Do you have any memory of what happened?"

She shook her head and pointed at the Sabbat Box. "He had me smell one of the vials. Like you just did. I was leery but, I have to say, the experience was marvelous. I had such vivid dreams. Images that worked their way into what he was doing to me. The combination of the drug and the domination totally soothed my nerves."

I realized her dilemma. Only the four of us knew about the video. I'd not told Marcher, revealing only that I knew something extremely damaging. The three of us would keep silent. But Denton? No way. I pointed toward him. "He's working for Casimir. He won't keep your secret."

She nodded, agreeing with the assessment.

"But you have it wrong. He's not trying to embarrass me," she said, her voice low. "It's more complicated than that."

I understood. "He wants something?"

The conflict within her eyes seemed to resolve itself. "I have damaging information on President Casimir. Proof that Casimir accepted fifty million euros from Libya, money he used to finance his first election. It came straight from Muammar Gaddafi, when he was still in power. He was buying EU protection through France."

"Is there proof?" I asked.

She nodded. "The man who delivered the money is willing to come forward. We've taken a sworn statement from him. We then traced the money, following the trail he provided. Casimir took the payoff personally and we've found the accounts in Liechtenstein and Switzerland. That amount would be twice the legal limit of twenty-one million euros allowed for any campaign. It also violates our foreign financing laws and campaign disclosure rules. This is way beyond a few dirty tricks or some character assassination. We were planning on revealing the information during the debate."

Which explained Denton's timing.

"Casimir, after winning five years ago, brought Gaddafi to France for a state visit and treated him like a respected leader. Most thought it odd at the time, but excused it as part of diplomacy. Ultimately, Casimir turned on his benefactor and allowed France to participate in NATO-led airstrikes that helped rebels overthrow Gaddafi. Of course, Gaddafi being killed during the Libyan revolution silenced him forever. But witnesses remain. The money was circulated through Casimir's campaign. People knew. Now I know."

"So Denton was looking for something Casimir could use as leverage?" Antoine asked.

St. Benedict nodded. "Your brother knew I was going to reveal this at the debate. So I imagine there would have been a trade. My secret for Casimir's. Mine is a bit more benign, but I need the right and the far-right to win this election, and my sexual proclivities would make their support hard to cement. The revelation on me would be as devastating as the one on Casimir."

"I can deal with Denton." She seemed interested in my declaration. "Only the two of you are aware of your *private* situation?"

"That portion of my house is known only to me, and those I allow inside. Which have been few. Four, to be precise. Three of whom I would stake my life on their discretion. Denton was the fourth."

"That means it's containable." I closed my eyes and tried once again to envision the dream. Particularly, the workshop. The racks of bottles. The three lined on the table. Everything seemed foggy. Unclear. Difficult to recall. Then clarity arrived. I moved toward the Sabbat Box and found the same three bottles, lying them on the coffee table.

"I need a glass."

St. Benedict brought one to me. I uncorked the bottles and poured a small amount of each into the glass, not worried about the fumes. I knew these worked in a different way, or at least that's what happened in the dream. I swirled the contents into a mixture.

"Open his shirt," I said to Antoine.

He ripped the buttons clear and exposed his brother's chest. I poured the contents of the glass onto his skin. The sensation awoke Denton with a start. He stared at us hard, unable to speak, then his eyes rolled skyward and his head fell to one side.

Like Kaz in the bath.

Antoine held him upright.

"Lay him down," I said.

I moved away, still holding the glass. We all watched as Denton lay still.

"How did you know about the mixture," St. Benedict asked.

"I saw it in the past."

"What if you're wrong?" she asked. "What if it kills him?"

"It won't." I knew that for sure, which was strange.

St. Benedict sat in a chair. "This is all too much. You say there's a video on that phone of me. I suppose this is my own fault. I seemed to have misplaced my trust."

"Denton is good at exploiting other people's weaknesses," Antoine said.

"He was so charming. So smart. He's been a great asset. But, I assume, that was all part of the act." St. Benedict paused. "I'm not ashamed of what I find enjoyable, but that's a private matter. Only for me. It hurts no one. But my children. I would not want them to see any of that. They are far too young to understand."

The change in the timbre of her voice signaled sadness.

"I want to lead this country. I'm the best choice to lead this country. Sadly, though, this could cost me the chance. Denton was right about one thing. It won't take much to alter the results."

"It's under control now," I told her.

"You seem so sure."

"I need to rinse this glass out."

She pointed to a door and I found a bathroom. There, I washed out the inside, then filled it with water. I returned to where Antoine lay and did exactly as Morgan had done with Kaz, splashing the water onto Denton's face and chest.

He stirred, groaning.

Antoine bent down to help his brother sit up.

Denton returned to reality, blinking his eyes into focus. "Antoine. What's going on?"

Brother faced brother.

"What do you remember?" Antoine asked.

Denton seemed to consider the question hard. Then, he said, "That we need to be at the estate. There's work to be done. Where's Father?"

The tone was totally different. Nothing threatening, nor arrogant. Much more like Antoine. Now for the ultimate test.

"Do you know who I am?" I asked him.

Denton shook his head. "I have no idea."

"And this woman?" I pointed to Lydia St. Benedict. "Do you know her?"

He shook his head. "Should I?"

Chapter 18

I PARKED AT THE BOTTOM OF THE MOUNTAIN IN THE PUBLIC SPOTS reserved for visitors to Eze, back where it all started. The candidates' debate happened last night and Lydia St. Benedict had shown herself as presidential, especially when she dropped the bomb about Casimir's Libyan connection. It had come in reply to a question about competency for office and Casimir had denied the allegation, which only fueled speculation. The media had exploded after and continued all night. The Casimir campaign was in a free fall. Prosecutors had already publicly stated that an investigation would be opened. Both candidates were headed back out on the campaign trail today, but Casimir's task had become much more difficult.

Marcher had taken charge of the silver cell phone and found an expert who was able to break through its password. Denton, changed by the potion, was no help as he had zero memory of anyone or anything for the past decade. The video from the dungeon had been stored on the silver phone, with no record of it being sent to anyone. Apparently St. Benedict had been right and Denton was waiting a little longer before springing his surprise. He'd assumed that I was no longer a threat, dead from the bottle in the Sabbat Box. No evidence existed that the Casimir campaign had the video, proven by the fact that no mention of it had been made at the debate or after.

Antoine and Denton had also left Paris, traveling to the Lussac estate in southern France. The potion had caused Denton's mind to revert back to a personality that existed when their father was alive. A totally different man, as Antoine had explained. One he liked. I was happy for the brothers. Things were definitely different for them.

And with me.

I climbed the steep path to the village. Sunlight peeked through the leafy canopy, spotting the ground with shadows. It was a lovely day with only a few white rags of clouds stretching across a blue dome of sky. Far different than two days ago with all the rain. A lot had happened over the past forty-eight hours. I'd experienced something that could not be real, yet it seemed nothing short of that. I'd known exactly which ingredients to use from the box, how to mix them, and what the concoction could do. Shocking, considering I had no training in chemistry. The only way the information could have been acquired was through the dream. The whole thing remained troubling. I'd called Cotton and told him what happened, explaining the outcome, even telling him more about the dreams. I had not wanted to say anything at first. But we had a rule. No secrets. God knows we'd broken it enough in the early stages of our relationship. But no longer. We kept nothing from each other. Or at least nothing significant. Cotton, god bless him, had not tried to tell me I was hallucinating.

Quite the opposite.

"You and I have both been involved with some pretty weird stuff," he said. *"Things we had a tough time explaining. So roll with it."*

He was right.

Which was why I'd returned to Eze.

I entered the village and followed the twisting cobbles to the same familiar back corner and the Museum of Mysteries. Nicodème answered my knock and invited me inside. He'd already brewed a steaming pot of green tea and had cheese and crackers prepared. I'd called earlier and said I was coming. He too was eager to know what had happened. We sat at a table and I told him everything. I was especially explicit about the hallucinations since, if anyone could explain them, he could.

"It has to be nonsense," I told him.

"Why?"

"You can't be serious. Past lives? Reincarnation? Morgan le Fay? She's merely a part of the Arthurian fiction."

He smiled. "There's more to her than you know."

Coming from anyone else I'd be skeptical, but I knew Nicodème dabbled in things most people found fantastical.

"Whenever I visit St. Margaret's Church, in London," he said, "I always linger at the east window. It's a magnificent stained-glass depiction, crafted in Flanders at the command of Ferdinand and Isabella in 1501 to celebrate the marriage of their daughter, Catherine of Aragon, to Arthur, the eldest son of the English king, Henry VII. Henry had been so fascinated with the Arthurian legend that he named his heir after him."

I knew that fact.

"After ending the Wars of the Roses, and killing Richard III, Henry VII, the first Tudor king, was intent on resurrecting the English throne through his issue, and he wanted it to start with Arthur. Unfortunately, his son died young, shortly after the marriage, even before the window in St. Margaret's arrived on English soil. Poor Catherine eventually married Arthur's brother, Henry VIII, and went on to suffer the disgrace of a forced divorce and an early death.

"Most have no understanding the significance Arthur holds for the English. Imagine if the American, George Washington, was merely a legend. Something only poets spoke about. Would not proving him real have meaning? A great significance? Arthur is the bridge that binds the ancient Brits to the modern English."

"I hear what you're saying, but I can't accept that those dreams were of something real."

He chuckled. "It's that analytical, engineering mind of yours. It makes you such a skeptic. But you've been privy to something few will ever know. A view to a past life."

But I still wasn't sure. "I remember the story. How Arthur lost his sword in a fight with Sir Pellinore. He asked Merlin what to do and the wizard guided him to water. The Lady of the Lake then gives Arthur a sword, the finest in all the world, and as long as he wears the scabbard nothing can harm him."

He nodded. "A wondrous tale. And much of that is pure fiction. But most good fiction is based in fact. And this is no exception. Come with me."

I stood from the table and followed him to the rear of the shop, past the oak paneled door bound by iron that led deeper into the mountain and the museum itself. I knew that only Nicodème could open it through an ancient puzzle. No one had ever seen that happen and I doubted anyone ever would, until he selected an apprentice. Beyond the door, in a square, dark-paneled room on a trestle table, lay a small book about the size of a prayer missal. Definitely old, but in respectable condition. On the cover were five words, the script no more than shadows in places.

De excidio et conquestu Britanniae.

"Concerning the Ruin and Conquest of Britain," he said, pointing at the volume. "This is a Gildas manuscript."

I knew that name.

Gildas Sapiens.

Who lived in Britain during the 6th century and penned a scathing attack on his contemporary churchmen and rulers. His words, a history of post-Roman, pre-St. Augustine, Britain, were a denunciation of secular and ecclesiastical authority. Most historians regarded his observations as more fiction than fact. But they remained the only firsthand account of 6th century Britain. Nothing else had survived.

"There are about seventy editions of his work still around," he said. "I'm always amused at the one in the British Museum. It's a 10th century handwritten copy of an 8th century text. Not nearly as authentic as they would want people to believe."

I smiled. "Double hearsay?"

"Precisely. This is an original. Maybe the only one left in the world."

I was impressed. But there was a lot about the Museum of Mysteries that fit into that category.

"Gildas was definitely biased, but he was also an ardent observer, a political critic in a time when criticism was not tolerated." He opened the top cover. "It's on vellum. Much better than parchment or papyrus. Which is why it has lasted."

I studied the pages.

The sheets rested on top of one another individually with no binding, the vellum waffled from time. Each still possessed a creamy white patina, an almost unused look, the writing faded to a light gray, the penmanship small and tight, the words running the entire length with no paragraphs or punctuation.

"They didn't believe in margins?" I asked.

"Writing materials were too precious. Every bit of a surface was used."

"Can you read it?"

He nodded. "It's old Latin. It talks of a man named Arturius."

A shiver snaked down my spine.

"He was a Roman who lived in the 6th century. A real person. Not a work of fiction. Unfortunately, it's a tainted record."

I listened as he explained.

He lifted off more sheets. "Listen to this passage. *Arturius fell at the battle of Camlan. He gave orders that he be taken to Venodocia so that he may sojourn on the Isle of Avalon for the sake of peace and for the easing of his wounds.* Venodocia was later called Gwynedd, an actual kingdom that spread across North Wales. This manuscript confirms Avalon was a place, in that locale, just as the poets eventually mused."

He explained that, until the 12th century, a character named Arthur was known only in bardic tales and Welsh poems. But Geoffrey of Monmouth changed everything in 1136 when he translated the *History of the Kings of Britons,* a fanciful account, more fiction than reality, that elevated Arthur into a king. The story was immensely popular. Three hundred years later, when Sir Thomas Malory finally wrote his famous epic, *Le Morte d'Arthur,* the character was forever ingrained into the realm of myth.

"But that Arthur was based on a real man," Nicodème said. "Not the chivalric character Malory envisioned. Not at all. Instead, Gildas shows us he was a brutal, barbarous man who fought Saxons, not unlike a thousand other warrior leaders who arose during the Dark Ages. There was no concept of kingship in Britain then. Just local chieftains who led men. Arturius was fortunate that later poets saw something more in his life. So they manufactured a legend."

I continued to stare at the vellum pages.

Windows to another time too.

"And it worked," Nicodème said. "So many English kings tried to make the Arthur connection. Edward I called himself *Arthurus Redivivus*—Arthur Returned. In the 13th century King John killed his nephew, named Arthur, who should have succeeded to the throne. John's father, Henry II, wanted his successor to bear the name. More recently, Prince William named his second son Louis Arthur Charles."

"What about Morgan le Fay," I asked.

"She was real too."

He turned over a few more pages. "Gildas says she was called by many names. Morgen, Morgaine, Morganna, Morgne. He mentions her as a great healer, one who became a dangerous enemy of Arturius. He called her Modron. To the later poets she became Arthur's half-sister. But who's to say she wasn't based on someone real? In Malory's *Le Morte d'Arthur* she's an apprentice of Merlin and a vindictive adversary of Arthur, with a special hatred for his wife Queen Guinevere."

I recalled from the dream how Arturius' wife felt about Morgan.

Not good.

"For Malory, in his tale, she was also wanton and sexually aggressive, with many lovers."

Another truth from the visions.

"My dreams were more of Gildas than of the Arthur from the poets," I pointed out. "I've never read Malory."

"But you know enough of the poems that they surely affected how you saw the visions. You were inside Morgan's head. With her thoughts. But your thoughts were there too. Past life visions require patience and practice to understand. They can be both revealing and deceiving."

I was definitely confused.

"I need to show you something else," he said, leading me to another table where a large piece of red silk covered something. He removed the cloth to reveal a small bronze shield. On it was an etched image.

"This is from the 6th century, too," he said. "Verified by experts. It's original. I've had it here, in the museum, for a long time."

It was of a man. Thick featured, who cast a saturnine look of unbending determination. A scar ran from the hairline to the corner of his mouth and the eyes, captured so well by the artist, seemed foreboding. I noticed something uncompromising in his expression, a message from the pinched lips and tight jaw which seemed to say he was accustomed to being free. The dress was a knee-length tunic and breeches, leather jerkin with metal studded fringe across the abdomen, a cloak pinned at the shoulders with a broach.

"He's quite imposing," I said. "He looks Roman."

"Celtic warriors aped Roman parade dress."

"Who is this?"

"Arturius himself."

He turned the shield over. On the back side were words.

ARTVRIVS. SUPERBUS TYRANNUS.

"Arthur. Outstanding Ruler," he translated.

I traced the scar down the image's face with the tip of my forefinger. "Not the image Hollywood would create."

He chuckled. "Hardly. But, after all, he was a warrior first and foremost. A leader of men."

Something about him reminded me of Helians, whose face was still inside my head. I'd always thought Arthur something of fiction. But this was altogether different.

"Can all this be real?" I asked.

"Cassiopeia, Heinrich Schliemann proved Homer did not fantasize Troy. He found the actual place, along with its gold. You have to remember, Arthur was never mentioned in writing until the 8th century. Nothing exists of him prior to that. That's why most scholars say he was a fabrication. Nothing from his actual time ever refers to him."

"Except for your Gildas manuscript and Arturius."

"Precisely. And the similarity in name is not coincidental. Gildas counters all speculation. He tell us that Arturius was a man fighting for a cause, like a million other revolutionaries who came after him. He fought Saxons, but those same Saxons in 1066 battled invading Normans. Together, Saxons and Normans became the English. Then, in 1941, while repelling the Germans, they echoed that same fighting sentiment. Arturius, the man, is even better than the poet's Arthur."

"But what of Morgan," I asked. "She seems my connection to all of this."

He turned over a few more pages.

"There's not much here on her. But Gildas does quote a poem which mentions her." He found the passage. "Here it is. *But when Morgan with lifted hand, moved down the hall, they louted low. For she was Queen of Shadowland, that woman of snow.*"

I was shocked.

And nothing from my current memories would have skewed that vision, since I'd never heard those words before.

Not until the dreams.

"Is the author of the verse noted?" I asked.

He shook his head. "Nothing is mentioned."

But I knew.

Writer's Note

This story was a collaboration we've both wanted to do for a long time. It was fun to finally make it a reality. Cassiopeia Vitt comes from Steve's Cotton Malone series. And though she had her own short story with *The Balkan Escape*, this is her first foray into the realm of a novella. Who knows? Perhaps a full-length novel, with her as protagonist, is in her future. The story also utilized two characters from M.J.'s world, Jac L'Etoile and Pierre Marcher, and made mention of a third, Dr. Malachi Samuels. The rest of the cast are new to both writers.

Time now to separate the real from the imagined.

The Sabbat Box which appears throughout the story is an actual artifact. Ancient priests and priestesses kept their working ingredients inside one. People who were once labeled a witch would now be called a chemist or pharmacist, as both disciplines trace their origins to ancients who began to notice and appreciate the effects plants can have on the human body. All of the various items contained within the bottles that Cassiopeia comes in contact with are real substances.

The French village of Eze is a wondrous place. It sits atop a hill like something from another time. Though there should be, there is no Museum of Mysteries there. But all of the items detailed in chapter 1 that are supposedly inside the museum are from history. The Philosopher's Walk (chapter 1 and 5) is also there, the climb as arduous as described.

The tools of the perfume trade detailed in chapter 8 are accurate. Perfume forms a big part of M.J.'s stories.

The scandal utilized in chapter 17 involving our fictional President Casimir and Libya is based on actual charges filed against former French president Nicolas Sarkozy, who stood accused of accepting fifty million euros from Muammar Gaddafi. As of the time of the first release of this story, those charges are still pending.

Morgan le Fay is a fictional character from the Arthurian legends. Whether she was a real person no one knows, but there are accounts of women similar to her living all across ancient Britain. She's been called many names (chapter 18) and was believed to be a healer, an enchantress, and a mysterious woman with spiritual talents. In Thomas Malory's *Le Morte d'Arthur*, she became King Arthur's half-sister, unhappily married to King Urien. She's depicted as a sexually aggressive woman with many lovers, including the sorcerer Merlin. But her love for Lancelot stays unrequited. She also is an indirect cause of Arthur's death. Many times she's described as a witch. In later accounts of the Arthurian legend (which changed over time) she became an anti-heroine, noted as a malicious, cruel, and an ambitious nemesis of Arthur. Further evolution of the character changed her into Merlin's lover, who supposedly teaches her witchcraft. The poetry Helians recites to Morgan and Nicodème reads to Cassiopeia (chapters 16 and 18) is not ours. It is part of a larger poem, *Morgan le Fay*, by Madison Julius Cawein, who lived in the latter part of the 19th century.

The exploits of Arthur described in chapter 4 are also from the legend, but the information about him being based on a Saxon warrior leader (chapters 7 and 9) is not outside the realm of possibility. As detailed in chapters 2, 9, and 11, various kings have wanted to name their potential heirs Arthur, but death seemed always to interfere. Curiously, there has only been one King Arthur in all of English history.

The *History of the Kings of Britain* by Geoffrey of Monmouth and *On the Ruin and Conquest of Britain,* by Gildas, (chapter 18) are actual manuscripts. The addition of specific references to Arturius in the Gildas work was our invention. Of all the kings and queens who ruled England, only Arthur became a legend. But, as was noted in the story, whatever real life counterpart formed the basis of the fictional character, he was most likely not a king. Just a Celtic leader of men, fighting for what he believed in.

In closing, a few lines from Tennyson comes to mind. One of those later poets who improved on the Arthurian legend. It's from his *Idylls of the King,* at a point when Arthur lays dying from his wounds, about to embark on his final voyage to the isle of Avalon.

The words are fitting then and now:

The old order changeth, yielding place to new,
And God fulfils himself in many ways,
Lest one good custom should corrupt the world.
Comfort thyself: what comfort is in me?
I have lived my life, and that which I have done
May He within himself make pure!
If thou shouldst never see my face again,
Pray for my soul.

Sign up for the 1001 Dark Nights Newsletter
and be entered to win a Tiffany Lock necklace.

There's a contest every quarter!

Go to www.1001DarkNights.com to subscribe.

As a bonus, all subscribers will receive a free copy of
Discovery Bundle Three
Featuring stories by
Sidney Bristol, Darcy Burke, T. Gephart
Stacey Kennedy, Adriana Locke
JB Salsbury, and Erika Wilde

Discover 1001 Dark Nights Collection Five

For more information, visit www.1001DarkNights.com.

BLAZE ERUPTING by Rebecca Zanetti
Scorpius Syndrome/A Brigade Novella

ROUGH RIDE by Kristen Ashley
A Chaos Novella

HAWKYN by Larissa Ione
A Demonica Underworld Novella

RIDE DIRTY by Laura Kaye
A Raven Riders Novella

ROME'S CHANCE by Joanna Wylde
A Reapers MC Novella

THE MARRIAGE ARRANGEMENT by Jennifer Probst
A Marriage to a Billionaire Novella

SURRENDER by Elisabeth Naughton
A House of Sin Novella

INKED NIGHT by Carrie Ann Ryan
A Montgomery Ink Novella

ENVY by Rachel Van Dyken
An Eagle Elite Novella

PROTECTED by Lexi Blake
A Masters and Mercenaries Novella

THE PRINCE by Jennifer L. Armentrout
A Wicked Novella

PLEASE ME by J. Kenner
A Stark Ever After Novella

WOUND TIGHT by Lorelei James
A Rough Riders/Blacktop Cowboys Novella®

STRONG by Kylie Scott
A Stage Dive Novella

DRAGON NIGHT by Donna Grant
A Dark Kings Novella

TEMPTING BROOKE by Kristen Proby
A Big Sky Novella

HAUNTED BE THE HOLIDAYS by Heather Graham
A Krewe of Hunters Novella

CONTROL by K. Bromberg
An Everyday Heroes Novella

HUNKY HEARTBREAKER by Kendall Ryan
A Whiskey Kisses Novella

THE DARKEST CAPTIVE by Gena Showalter
A Lords of the Underworld Novella

Discover 1001 Dark Nights Collection One

For more information, visit www.1001DarkNights.com.

FOREVER WICKED by Shayla Black
CRIMSON TWILIGHT by Heather Graham
CAPTURED IN SURRENDER by Liliana Hart
SILENT BITE: A SCANGUARDS WEDDING by Tina Folsom
DUNGEON GAMES by Lexi Blake
AZAGOTH by Larissa Ione
NEED YOU NOW by Lisa Renee Jones
SHOW ME, BABY by Cherise Sinclair
ROPED IN by Lorelei James
TEMPTED BY MIDNIGHT by Lara Adrian
THE FLAME by Christopher Rice
CARESS OF DARKNESS by Julie Kenner

Also from 1001 Dark Nights

TAME ME by J. Kenner

Discover 1001 Dark Nights Collection Two

For more information, visit www.1001DarkNights.com.

Discover 1001 Dark Nights Collection Three

For more information, visit www.1001DarkNights.com.

HIDDEN INK by Carrie Ann Ryan
BLOOD ON THE BAYOU by Heather Graham
SEARCHING FOR MINE by Jennifer Probst
DANCE OF DESIRE by Christopher Rice
ROUGH RHYTHM by Tessa Bailey
DEVOTED by Lexi Blake
Z by Larissa Ione
FALLING UNDER YOU by Laurelin Paige
EASY FOR KEEPS by Kristen Proby
UNCHAINED by Elisabeth Naughton
HARD TO SERVE by Laura Kaye
DRAGON FEVER by Donna Grant
KAYDEN/SIMON by Alexandra Ivy/Laura Wright
STRUNG UP by Lorelei James
MIDNIGHT UNTAMED by Lara Adrian
TRICKED by Rebecca Zanetti
DIRTY WICKED by Shayla Black
THE ONLY ONE by Lauren Blakely
SWEET SURRENDER by Liliana Hart

Discover 1001 Dark Nights Collection Four

For more information, visit www.1001DarkNights.com.

ROCK CHICK REAWAKENING by Kristen Ashley
ADORING INK by Carrie Ann Ryan
SWEET RIVALRY by K. Bromberg
SHADE'S LADY by Joanna Wylde
RAZR by Larissa Ione
ARRANGED by Lexi Blake
TANGLED by Rebecca Zanetti
HOLD ME by J. Kenner
SOMEHOW, SOME WAY by Jennifer Probst
TOO CLOSE TO CALL by Tessa Bailey
HUNTED by Elisabeth Naughton
EYES ON YOU by Laura Kaye
BLADE by Alexandra Ivy/Laura Wright
DRAGON BURN by Donna Grant
TRIPPED OUT by Lorelei James
STUD FINDER by Lauren Blakely
MIDNIGHT UNLEASHED by Lara Adrian
HALLOW BE THE HAUNT by Heather Graham
DIRTY FILTHY FIX by Laurelin Paige
THE BED MATE by Kendall Ryan
PRINCE ROMAN by CD Reiss
NO RESERVATIONS by Kristen Proby
DAWN OF SURRENDER by Liliana Hart

Also from 1001 Dark Nights

TEMPT ME by J. Kenner

About the Authors

STEVE BERRY is the New York Times and #1 internationally bestselling author of fourteen Cotton Malone novels and four stand-alones. He has 23 million books in print, translated into 40 languages. With his wife, Elizabeth, he is the founder of History Matters, which is dedicated to historical preservation. He serves on the Smithsonian Libraries Advisory Board and was a founding member of International Thriller Writers, formerly serving as its co-president.

* * * *

New York Times bestseller, M.J. Rose grew up in New York City mostly in the labyrinthine galleries of the Metropolitan Museum, the dark tunnels and lush gardens of Central Park and reading her mother's favorite books before she was allowed. She believes mystery and magic are all around us but we are too often too busy to notice... books that exaggerate mystery and magic draw attention to it and remind us to look for it and revel in it.

Please visit her blog, Museum of Mysteries at http://www.mjrose.com/blog/

Rose's work has appeared in many magazines including *Oprah* magazine and she has been featured in the *New York Times, Newsweek, Wall Street Journal, Time, USA Today* and on the Today Show, and NPR radio. Rose graduated from Syracuse University, spent the '80s in advertising, has a commercial in the Museum of Modern Art in New York City and since 2005 has run the first marketing company for authors - Authorbuzz.com

Rose lives in Connecticut with her husband the musician and composer, Doug Scofield.

The Bishop's Pawn
A Cotton Malone Novel
By Steve Berry
Now Available

History notes that the ugly feud between J. Edgar Hoover and Martin Luther King, Jr., marked by years of illegal surveillance and the accumulation of secret files, ended on April 4, 1968 when King was assassinated by James Earl Ray. But that may not have been the case.

Now, fifty years later, former Justice Department agent, Cotton Malone, must reckon with the truth of what really happened that fateful day in Memphis.

It all turns on an incident from eighteen years ago, when Malone, as a young Navy lawyer, is trying hard not to live up to his burgeoning reputation as a maverick. When Stephanie Nelle, a high-level Justice Department lawyer, enlists him to help with an investigation, he jumps at the opportunity. But he soon discovers that two opposing forces—the Justice Department and the FBI—are at war over a rare coin and a cadre of secret files containing explosive revelations about the King assassination, information that could ruin innocent lives and threaten the legacy of the civil rights movement's greatest martyr.

Malone's decision to see it through to the end —— from the raucous bars of Mexico, to the clear waters of the Dry Tortugas, and ultimately into the halls of power within Washington D.C. itself —— not only changes his own life, but the course of history.

Here's an excerpt:

CHAPTER ONE

June
18 Years Ago

Two favors changed my life.

The first happened on a warm Tuesday morning. I was cruising on Southside Boulevard, in Jacksonville, Florida listening to the radio. A quick stab at the seek button and through the car speakers came, "Why does New York have lots of garbage and Los Angeles lots of lawyers?"

"New York got first choice?"

Laughter clamored, followed by, "How do you get a lawyer out of a tree?"

No one seemed to know the answer.

"Cut the rope."

"The other day terrorists hijacked an airliner full of lawyers."

"That's awful. What happened?"

"They threatened that unless their demands were met they would begin releasing one lawyer every hour."

More laughter.

"What do lawyers and—"

I turned the radio off. The disc jockeys seemed to be having fun, lawyers apparently a safe object of ridicule. Hell, who was going to complain? It wasn't like gay jokes, Polish jokes, or anything even remotely sexist. Everybody hated lawyers. Everybody told a lawyer joke. And if the lawyers didn't like it, who gave a damn?

Actually, I did.

Since I was a lawyer.

A good one in my opinion.

My name, Harold Earl "Cotton" Malone, appeared as one of thousands at the time who held a license within the State of Georgia, where I'd taken the bar exam six years earlier. But I'd never worked at any law firm. Instead I was a lieutenant commander in the U.S. Navy, assigned to the Judge Advocate General's corps, currently on duty at the naval station in Mayport, Florida. Today, though, I wasn't acting as a lawyer. Instead, I was doing a favor for a friend, a distraught husband going through a divorce.

A favor I was beginning to regret.

The wife, Sue Weiler, possessed the cunning of a dictator and the boldness of a stripper. She'd spent yesterday parading across Jacksonville from apartment to apartment. Four in all. Men she'd met here and there. Fast sex with no strings. While sitting outside Apartment Number 3 I'd seriously wondered if she might be a nymphomaniac, as she certainly possessed the appetite.

Just past 5:00, after a surprisingly brief visit at Apartment Number 4, she folded her long slender legs into a sparkling new Cadillac and headed onto a busy boulevard. The car was a rosy shade of white, so pale that it looked pink. I knew the story. She'd specially ordered the car to enrage her estranged husband, the stunt entirely consistent with her taunting personality.

Last night she'd headed straight to an apartment complex on the south side and Boyfriend Number 5. A month ago she'd done the same thing and, being the pal that I was, I'd followed her then, too. Now the soon-to-be-ex-husband's lawyer wanted pictures and, if possible, video to use in divorce court. My buddy had already been socked with temporary alimony, part of which was going to pay for the Cadillac. Proof of adultery would certainly stop all alimony. Especially since Sue had already twice testified that she possessed no lovers or hardly any male friends at all. She was an accomplished liar, and if I hadn't seen the truth myself I would have believed her.

A light rain had fallen all yesterday afternoon, and the evening had been typically hot and humid for Florida in June. I'd spent the night rooted outside the apartment of Boyfriend Number 5 making sure Sue didn't slip away. Fifteen minutes ago she'd emerged and sped off in the Pink Mobile. I speculated where she might be headed. An apartment complex out at the beach and Boyfriend Number 6, a title insurance agent with the advantage of forty pounds more muscle and twenty fewer years than her husband.

The morning was bright and sunny, the roads filled with commuters, Jacksonville traffic always challenging. My metallic blue Regal easily melded into the morning confusion, and following a nearly pink Cadillac presented little difficulty. Predictably, she took the same series of twists and turns across town until her left signal blinked and the Cadillac veered into another apartment complex.

I noted the time.

7:58 a.m.

Boyfriend Number 6 lived in Building C, Unit 5, with two assigned parking spaces, one for his late-model Mazda, the other for a guest. I'd discovered those details a few weeks ago. Half an hour from now, allowing plenty of opportunity for them to climb into the sack, I'd find a good spot to grab a little video and a few snapshots of the Cadillac beside the Mazda. In the meantime I'd wait across the street in a shopping center parking lot. To pass the time I had a couple of paperback novels.

I flipped on my right blinker and was just about to turn into the shopping center when a Ford pickup shot by in the left lane. I noticed the cobalt color, then the bumper sticker.

My ex-wife's new car is a broom.

And knew the occupant.

My pal, the soon-to-be-ex-husband.

I'd last talked to Bob Weiler at midnight, calling in the bad news, none of which he'd liked. Him being here now meant only one thing— trouble. I'd sensed a growing resentment for some time. The seemingly blasé attitude the wife took to her husband's jealousy. A delight in emotionally building him up, then enjoying while he crashed before her eyes. An obvious game of control. His for her affection, hers for the pleasure of being able to dictate his response. But such games carried risks and most times the participants could not care less about the consequences.

Bob's pickup, in defiance to some substantial onooming traffic, flew across the opposite lanes, tires squealing, and shot into the narrow drive, barely missing the carved cedar sign proclaiming the entrance to The Legends. I aborted my right turn, changed lanes and, taking advantage of some rubberneckers, followed. Traffic momentarily blocked my approach, and by the time I finally made the turn into the complex Bob was a good ninety seconds ahead of me.

I headed straight for Building C.

The truck was stopped, its driver's-side door open. The pink Cadillac sat parked beside the Mazda. Bob Weiler stood with a gun leveled at his wife, who'd emerged from her car but had yet to go inside. I whipped the steering wheel to the right and slammed the Regal into park. Groping through the glove compartment I found my Smith & Wesson .38 and hoped to God I didn't have to use it.

I popped open the door and slid out. "Put it down, Bob."

"No way, Cotton. I'm tired of this bitch playing me for a fool." Bob kept his gun trained on Sue. "Stay out of this. This is between me and her."

I stayed huddled behind my open car door and glanced left. Several residents watched the unfolding scene from railed balconies. I stole a quick look at the wife, fifty feet away. Not a hint of fear laced her gorgeous face. She actually looked more annoyed than anything else, watching her husband intently, the look reminiscent of a lioness surveying her prey. A stylish Chanel purse draped one shoulder.

I turned my attention back to Bob Weiler. "Put the gun down."

"This bitch is milking me while she screws whoever she wants."

"Let the divorce court handle her. We've got enough now."

He turned toward me. "The hell with courts. I can deal with this right now."

"For what? Prison? She's not worth it."

Two shots cracked in the morning air and Bob Weiler let out a groan, then his body crumpled to the ground. Blood poured from a pair of holes in his chest. My gaze darted toward Sue. Her gun was still raised, only now it was pointed at me.

Another shot exploded.

I dove into the Regal.

The driver's side window, where I'd just been crouched, exploded, spraying glass on me.

She fired again.

The front windshield spiderwebbed from the impact but did not splinter. I snapped open the passenger-side door and slid out onto the pavement. Now at least a whole car was between us. I sprang up, gun aimed, and screamed, "Drop the gun."

She ignored me and fired one more time.

I ducked and heard the bullet ricochet off the hood. I came up and sent a round her way, which pierced Sue's right shoulder. She recoiled, trying to keep her balance, then she dropped to the pavement, losing a grip on her weapon. I rushed over and kicked the pistol aside.

"You no-good piece of crap," she yelled. "You shot me."

"You're lucky I didn't kill you."

"You're going to wish you did."

I shook my head in disbelief.

Wounded and bleeding, but still venomous.

Three Duval County Sheriff's cars with flashing lights and screaming sirens entered the complex and closed in fast. Uniformed officers poured out, ordering me to drop my gun. All of their weapons were pointed my way, so I decided not to tempt fate and did as they asked.

"This bastard shot me," Sue screamed.

"On the ground," one of the cops said to me. "Now."

Slowly I dropped to my knees, then laid belly-first on the damp parking lot. Immediately, my arms were twisted behind my back, a knee pressed firm to my spine, and cuffs snapped onto my wrists.

So much for favor number one.

Tiffany Blues

By M.J. Rose

Coming August 7, 2018

New York, 1924. Twenty-four-year-old Jenny Bell is one of a dozen burgeoning artists invited to Louis Comfort Tiffany's prestigious artists' colony. Gifted and determined, Jenny vows to avoid distractions and romantic entanglements and take full advantage of the many wonders to be found at Laurelton Hall.

But Jenny's past has followed her to Long Island. Images of her beloved mother, her hard-hearted stepfather, waterfalls, and murder, and the dank hallways of Canada's notorious Andrew Mercer Reformatory for Women overwhelm Jenny's thoughts, even as she is inextricably drawn to Oliver, Tiffany's charismatic grandson.

As the summer shimmers on, and the competition between the artists grows fierce as they vie for a spot at Tiffany's New York gallery, a series of suspicious and disturbing occurrences suggest someone knows enough about Jenny's childhood trauma to expose her.

Supported by her closest friend Minx Deering, a seemingly carefree socialite yet dedicated sculptor, and Oliver, Jenny pushes her demons aside. Between stolen kisses and stolen jewels, the champagne flows and the jazz plays on until one moonless night when Jenny's past and present are thrown together in a desperate moment, that will threaten her promising future, her love, her friendships, and her very life.

"A lush, romantic historical mystery with a unique setting. Tiffany Blues explores an interesting lost bit of American history and gives us a heroine to root for."—**Kristin Hannah, New York Times bestselling author of The Nightingale and The Great Alone**

Here's an excerpt:

Prologue
March 13, 1957
Laurelton Hall, Laurel Hollow
Oyster Bay, New York

I lost my heart long before this fire darkened its edges. I was twenty-four years old that once-upon-a-time summer when I fell in love.

A love that opened a door into a new world. A profusion of greens, shades of purples, spectrums of yellows, oranges, reds, and blues—oh, so many variations of blues.

I never dreamed I'd come back to Laurelton Hall, but I always trusted it would be there if I ever could visit. Now that will be impossible. For all that is left of that arcadia is this smoldering, stinking mess.

Somewhere in this rubble of charred trees, smashed tiles, and broken glass is my bracelet with its heart-shaped diamond and benitoite charm. Did my heart burn along with the magical house, the primeval forest, the lush bushes, and the glorious flowers? I'm not sure. Platinum is a hard metal. Diamonds are harder still. Or did just the engraving melt? And what of the man whose hand had grabbed at the bracelet? His muscle and flesh would have rotted by now. But what of the bones? Do bones burn? Back when it all happened, no report about a missing artist was ever made.

I take a few tentative steps closer to the rubble of the house. Bits of glass glint in the sun. A shard of ruby flashes, another of deep amethyst. I bend and pick up a fragment the size of my hand and wipe the soot off its surface.

With a start, I recognize this pattern.

Patterns, Mr. Tiffany once said, be they found in events, in nature, even in the stars in the firmament, are proof of history repeating itself. If we see randomness, it is only because we don't yet recognize the pattern.

So it shouldn't surprise me that of all the possible patterns, this is the one I've found. This remnant of the stained-glass clematis windows from Oliver's room. I remember how the light filtered through those windows, radiating color like the gems Mr. Tiffany used in his jewelry. How we stood in that living light and kissed, and the world opened up for me like an oyster, offering one perfect, luminous pearl. How that kiss became one more, then a hundred more. How we discovered each other's tastes and scents. How we shared that alchemical reaction when our passions ignited, combusted, and exploded, changing both of us forever.

Clutching the precious memory, I continue walking through the hulking mass of wreckage, treading carefully on the broken treasures. I listen for the familiar sounds—birds chirping, water splashing in the many fountains, and the endless rushing of the man-made waterfall that I always went out of my way to avoid.

But everything here is silent. Not even the birds have returned yet.

I learned about the fire seven days ago. I was at home in Paris, having breakfast, eating a croissant, drinking a café crème, and reading the *International*
Herald Tribune. The headline popped out at me like the obituary of an old friend with whom I had long been out of touch.

Old Tiffany Mansion Burns

An eight-level structure with twenty-five baths, the house was owned originally by the late Louis Comfort Tiffany of the jewelry firm that bears his name. At one time the estate covered 1,500 acres of woodland and waterfront.

I didn't realize my hand was shaking until I saw a splotch of coffee soak into my white tablecloth.

The structure later housed the Tiffany Art Foundation, which operated a summer school for artists.

The reporter wrote that a neighbor out walking his dog noticed flames coming from the clock tower of Laurelton's main house. Within hours, the mansion was ablaze. Fire companies came from as far as Hicksville and Glen Cove. Firemen drained all the neighboring swimming pools using the water to try to contain the conflagration. They carried hoses a half mile down to the Long Island Sound to siphon off that water, too. At one point, 435 firemen worked on the blaze, but the fire raged on and on for five days, defeating them. Those who lived nearby said the skies blackened as metal and wood, foliage, ephemera, and fabric burned.

The sky here is no longer black. But the smell of the fire persists. And no wonder, considering it burned for so long.

Once the present turns to past, all we have left are memories. Yes, sometimes we can stand where we stood, see our ghost selves, and relive moments of our life. See the shadow of the man we loved. Of the friend we cherished. Of the mentor who made all the difference. Our memories turn specific. The terrier that played by the shoreline, joyously running in the sand. We can remember the smell of the roses. Look at the azure water and see the glimmer of the sun on the opposite shore and hear a fleeting few bars of jazz still lingering in the air.

If you were the only girl in the world . . . Staring into the remains of what is left, I see ghosts of the gardens and woods, the gazebo, terraces, rooms ablaze with stained glass—everywhere we walked and talked and kissed and cried. With my eyes closed, I see it all in my mind, but when I open them, all of it is gone, up in flames.

Mr. Tiffany once told me that there is beauty even in broken things. Looking back, there is no question I would not be the artist I am if not for that lesson. But would he be able to salvage any beauty out of this destruction?

No, I never dreamed I'd come back to Laurelton Hall. The Xanadu where I came of age as both a woman and a painter. Where I found my heart's desire and my palette's power. Where depravity bloomed alongside beds and fields of flowers, where creativity and evil flowed with the water in the many fountains. Where the sun shone on the tranquil sea and the pool's treacherous rock crystals reflected rainbows onto the stone patio. Where the glorious light streaming from Mr. Tiffany's majestic stained glass illuminated the very deep darkness that had permeated my soul and lifted me out of despair. And where I found the love that sustained me and remained in my heart even after Oliver and I parted.

Standing here, smelling the acrid stench, looking at the felled trees with their charcoal bark, the carbon-coated stones and bent metal frames that once held the master's windows, at the smoky, melting mess that was one of the greatest mansions on Long Island's Gold Coast, I know I never will see it again, not how it was that magical and awful summer of 1924.

The fire is still hot in spots, and a tree branch snaps. My reverie is broken. Leaves rustle. Rubble falls. Glass crushes. Twigs crack. Then comes a whisper.

Jenny.

But it can't be. The wind howling through a hollow tree trunk is playing a trick. Fooling me into thinking I am hearing his sapphire voice, its deep velvet tone.

As I listen to the repeated whisper—*Jenny*—I raise my hand to wipe at my tears and tell myself that it is the smoldering ash making my eyes water. The charms on my bracelet jingle as I lower my arm. And again the whisper . . . and again my name—*Jenny.*

On behalf of 1001 Dark Nights,

Liz Berry and M.J. Rose would like to thank ~

Steve Berry
Doug Scofield
Kim Guidroz
Jillian Stein
InkSlinger PR
Dan Slater
Asha Hossain
Chris Graham
Fedora Chen
Kasi Alexander
Jessica Johns
Dylan Stockton
Richard Blake
Simon Lipskar

CPSIA information can be obtained
at www.ICGtesting.com
Printed in the USA
LVHW02s1839180718
584219LV00004B/519/P